HAD HE WORN A DIFFERENT BODY?

AND 20 OTHER UNEXPECTED TALES

BRAD ASHMORE

Cover illustration and design by Steven J. Catizone
Interior design by Megan McCullough

Copyright © 2018 Bradley Charles Ashmore

Published by Unexpected Books

TABLE OF CONTENTS

INTRODUCTION

These tales cover a diverse set of fiction genres and themes, making each one "unexpected". Five comprise a set of soft sci-fi tales that involve two characters named Amanda and Carl; their names appear in the title or by the second sentence. The other 16 tales are independent: Soft sci-fi, humor, absurd, or literary fiction.

My heartfelt thanks go to those who reviewed the stories and provided feedback: My wife, Leslie, and my children, Tom and Anne; also Stephanie Diaz and Alex Acks. Their objectivity was precious.

This project was difficult to conclude because of the mania to revisit and revise. But the time has come to publish. I hope that you find some unexpected enjoyment in this book.

Brad Ashmore
February 5, 2018

HAD HE WORN A DIFFERENT BODY?

SATURDAY AMBUSHED ROBERT LIKE A TRAPDOOR. WHO WAS HE going to wear to the party? He sighed, feeling so settled in the supple leather chair. The adjacent fireplace crackled. Resolved, he snapped the book shut, drummed his fingers on its stiff cover as he stared through it, and then placed it on the polished table beside the chair. He sprung out of his chair and briskly paced out of his library with an agility that belied his 83 years. After double-stepping up the marble staircase, he strode across the master suite toward the mahogany walk-in closet.

Swinging open its doors, he stepped in and was surrounded by a full wardrobe that covered every occasion. Weddings, corporate functions, birthday parties… there were body units for each type of affair and many of those affairs had played out at the same venue as tonight, The Foundation Club. He stood and gazed around at them, smiling at the memories they conjured: Chester's hilarious New Year's toast, Roger's tall tale at the board meeting, or the dance with MaryLou at the sales conference. *Hmmm... MaryLou will be there tonight*, he thought. *Maybe I should wear the same one as before. Which one was it?*

Like the rest, it was a fit man about 25-30 years old, but this one had rather broad shoulders. He recalled that it had come from the DNA of a handsome young tourist. DNA was so easy to capture—was it fingerprints that time?—and then the seed would be grown. A wardrobe grown over a generation. After all those years, why hadn't someone else thought of this yet? He supposed it was like his other inventions, the public ones, his deep well of funds: People were too distracted by what mattered today rather than what was possible. A shame.

Returning to the task at hand, he glanced down at a screen showing images of more units in storage. He scrolled through images until he fixed his eyes on the unit that danced with Mary Lou. He had worn that body for longer than most—a year? You get used to a body after a while, he thought. You get used to the smiles! *And it isn't murder if the bodies were never, well, alive,* he reminded himself. *Immortality doesn't have to be a zero sum game.*

He pressed "Select" next to the image. Like clothes hanging from a dry cleaner's conveyor, the wardrobe of body units glided past and then halted, gently swinging, when the chosen one hung before Robert. "That's it!" he said, smiling with a faraway look as a vision for the night began to form.

Robert sat in the transplant chair and, after a verbal "move body" command, a hood lowered over his head and filled with a sweet narcotic that brought a comatose sleep. Surgical snaps were automatically opened, linkages and sockets were released, and Robert's brain was deftly lifted out and transported to the receiving body unit. A reciprocal process plugged him into the new host, safe and sound. Current was applied, fluids flowed, and the body animated.

Secure in his new body, Robert stood and stretched to work out all of the little kinks. This one felt more vital than the previous one; as he breathed he could feel deep lung capacity and the beating of a strong heart. He walked into the mirrored alcove and gazed with approval at the surrounding images of himself, a new man. "Very nice," he said, slightly startled by the new gravelly baritone. Robert combed the generous wavy raven hair that concealed the snaps. He adjusted his tie and cufflinks and then called for his transport.

But as he turned to leave the closet he was stabbed by a sudden doubt. He had forgotten something, a key step in the re-personalization process. Behind a young though furrowed brow, his beleaguered 83-year-old mind searched. He likened his memory to an old fashioned Rolodex, stuffed with yellow dog-eared cards. Over time, cards could tatter and fall out to flitter down the dark dustbin of permanent forgetfulness.

"Wallet!" he exclaimed. His face beamed with relief that this precious Rolodex card was intact. He turned back and stepped toward a set of drawers built into the heavy, richly polished mahogany paneling. Grabbing a pair of brass knobs, he pulled open the drawer in which the wallets were stored. Once upon a time, they had been carefully cataloged, indexed by body unit. Today, they were in a cluttered heap. Robert shook his head at this further evidence of the insidious spread of his life's entropy.

A chime sounded the pending arrival of the summoned transport. "Dammit!" Robert grabbed a random wallet and tucked it into his vest pocket. "Oh, what the hell difference does it make?" He knew he had gotten sloppy maintaining a unique name for each body unit. *But, good grief, it's like having a name for each change of clothes!*

Robert glided down the staircase and then paused briefly to compose himself. "Pull it together, boy, pull it together." After a couple stabilizing deep breaths, he confidently strode to the entryway, swung open the great door, and boarded the transport.

Within an hour, the vehicle floated to the front of the palatial Foundation Club. He climbed out of the vehicle, which drifted away, and then strode through the broad entrance into the hall. Wearing this body, he didn't expect anyone else in tonight's crowd except MaryLou to recognize him. He was proficient at smooth-talking through the awkward moments when his invitation was challenged. Tonight, it was, "Oh shoot, I left the invitation in my transport!" accentuated by a forlorn gesture toward the rapidly departing vehicle. With an ingratiating smile and handshake, he was admitted, whereupon he began to scout for MaryLou.

Like a shorebird scanning for minnows that dart among the rocks, his eyes briskly swept and characterized the actors at every table. He waded into a deepening tide of clatter, music, laughter, and the mild roar of conversations. The air was warm, people were dancing or comfortably seated, introductions had been made, contacts established, and all were settled in for the duration. And then a melodic laugh signaled that she was here.

"MaryLou!" he called toward the trim redhead. She was in her mid-20s, similar to Robert's body, and leaned against the bar, martini propped by a wobbly arm. She strained to maintain a fixed gaze on the patient man standing beside her, the patient man whose 30 minutes of bar equity were about to crash.

Robert marched toward her, arms widening, face beaming. She pivoted around and cocked her head, causing the wobbly arm to deposit the remains of the martini on the patient man, and managed, "Whooo are you?"

Unable to recall the name of his body unit, he impulsively answered with his own, "Why, I'm Robert! Robert Tabbinot." He displaced the patient man who signaled a *good luck, brother* look as he brushed off his suit and, with some relief, left the bar.

MaryLou's face scrunched, exaggerated, quizzical. "Who'yer trying to fool?" she slurred. "I *know* Robert Tabby Not and R-Robert has sandy blond hair and isss just a *bit* taller than you." She had pinched her fingers together and smiled broadly to accentuate the "bit." She giggled, raising her non-martini'd hand several inches above Robert's head. "Up there... Nicer voice, too," she insisted.

Robert followed the hand up, but kept staring up as the hand came down, looking for a memory amongst the chandeliers and rising smoke. He obviously had already used his name, but for which body? Who was she describing? Had he worn a different body when he met MaryLou?

"Hey, down here, bub," she called after trying, but failing, to snap her fingers. "Buy a girl a drink?" She inverted the now empty glass and looked up at him with a pout.

Robert removed his wallet, turning her pout to a smile, but the smile promptly twisted into a smirk when she saw that the face on the driver's license didn't match the bearer.

Dammit! He snapped the wallet shut but that didn't stop the bewilderment over its contents, nor the mystery body unit he was wearing. Try as he might, all he could conjure were Rolodex cards spiraling into pitch darkness. The cascade of inconsistencies gathered into an avalanche of doubt that shook him to the core. *What did the original Robert look like?*

"Looks like you need a drink more than I do," said MaryLou as she turned, steadied herself, and slowly meandered to her next victim.

Robert caught his reflection in a window. He stood, stiffly staring at the young man; then Robert shuddered as his assumed reflection suddenly walked away.

What was happening? He had worn different bodies from his collection for years and changed with ease to suit the mood or situation. More than a change of clothing, wearing another body was a change of personhood. Up until tonight, he had managed this well, adopting a lifestyle to be anyone to everyone. But, after this unbroken chain of impersonations, he suddenly felt adrift; the long chain that connected to his authentic self was broken. This realization chilled his spine, or, rather, the spine of the anonymous person he now wore.

He searched for another familiar face, someone, *anyone*, who could help him to get his bearings. As he wandered the floor, his body no longer had the intimate sense of being part of him; he felt like a passenger in someone else's skin. Glancing down, disembodied shoes strode and carried Robert passively above them. He could make them stop, turn, and proceed as he wished but the messages were somehow relayed via an intermediary, someone or something other than Robert himself. The queer sensation soured his stomach and he directed his feet toward an open space on a sofa next to two other partygoers. His body sat.

A waiter passed by and Robert, shaking, reached up for a flute of champagne. He tried not to draw undue attention but the graying man sitting next to him noticed the unsteady glass aiming for Robert's mouth. "Hey, kid, are you OK?"

"Sure. Fine. I just need to steady my nerves a bit." Robert forced a smile. "Never seem to have the courage to ask a lady to dance... you know how it is."

The man smiled, but kept his gaze. Then he slightly tilted his head as recognition dawned. "This is going to sound odd, but would you be Mitch Campbell's son?"

"Hmm?" said Robert.

"Mitch Campbell was a good buddy of mine back in college and, by God, you are the spitting image," came the reply, hand outstretched to shake.

Robert took the hand, partly out of reflex but, ominously, because he couldn't recall the name of his body. "Yes," said Robert.

The man continued, "I'm Gordon Shultz; Gordie to your dad. Hey, you polished up pretty well! Nice threads! Better than your old man!" he said, laughing.

Like panning for gold, Robert sought some grain of truth to anchor a sentence. Finding none, he stood and replied, "Yes, well, I got lucky. Nice seeing you. I'll tell my dad that I met his old friend, uh, Gordie."

Before Gordon could follow up, Robert maneuvered toward the entrance and summoned the concierge for his transport. The concierge, who was completing a call, looked at the ticket and said, "It's going to be a bit of a wait." The call ended, he continued, "I hear there is quite a fire in Emerald Hills."

Robert stared at him, eyes furrowed. "That's where my home is."

Waving the ticket, the concierge said, "Right, that's why I told you." Another call stole his attention away.

Robert paced, hands in his pockets, watching transports arrive and depart for other destinations. Suddenly, he broke into a sprint and, pushing aside a couple preparing to enter a transport, he climbed in and shut the door. He shouted his address and the robotic vehicle proceeded, while calmly stating, "For public safety, this vehicle cannot pass the gates to Emerald Hills. Is that acceptable?"

"Yes! Yes! Of course!" he replied. His house was just two blocks inside the community.

As the transport approached its destination, Robert saw, with sickening dread, an expanding orange glow. Nearer, flames could be seen leaping over the silhouetted treetops into the night sky. The vehicle stopped at the gate and, as he stepped out, Robert heard the cacophony of sirens, hollering voices, and bullhorns over the background roar of the conflagration.

He sprinted the two blocks toward his home and then staggered as he confronted the scene. His mansion was belching smoke and flame.

He surged through a line of firefighters who were taken by surprise. "Hey, you can't go in there!" shouted one of the crew.

Robert turned, yelling, "I live here! I need my... medicine! It's a matter of life or death!" He sprinted ahead as the crew scrambled to respond.

Robert swung open the front door and pushed through the smoke, covering his mouth with his sleeve. He found the stairs and, eyes starting to sting, made his way up to the top, to his suite, and across to the closet. The air was thankfully clear inside and he shut the door to keep out the smoke. Time was of the essence. There was still power but he had to act fast. He activated the conveyor and body units began slowly drifting past.

Glass crashed outside and he could hear distant yelling. A seemingly endless cascade of body units, all men in their 20s and 30s, floated past. More sirens screamed, muted by the soft humanoid contours of the closeted space. Finally, the end of the train turned the corner and came into view. There he was... a gray, balding body. "Oh lord," uttered Robert, in distaste. It had been so many years since he saw the end of the line, or, more accurately, the beginning, for he was staring at the body of Robert Tabbinot.

A sudden vibration shook the structure, followed by a crash nearer than the others. Against the impending collapse of the house, Robert stared at the empty face on the body. He carefully considered this next step as the first wisps of smoke leaked into the closet. Was he really done with the years of impersonation, of youth worn like an expensive suit, inauthentic, and tailored to camouflage?

Taking a breath, he coughed, and then declared: "No more hiding."

Robert steered his old form to the transplant chair. He took his place in the other chair and, as lights flickered, he issued the command.

Outside the house, great arcs of water doused the structure that was losing its battle with the devouring flames. Vast orange clouds of smoke curled skyward, punctuated by an upward rain of brilliant sparks. "He hasn't come out yet! Suit up and go find him!" commanded the fire marshal to one of the crew. At that moment, a much older man emerged from the side of the house, limping, waving with one hand while the other covered his mouth.

"Wait!" said the fire marshal.

"That's not him!" yelled the firefighter over the roar of the flames and the machinery. "The one who ran in was a young guy."

Before the commander could speak, the old man shouted, coughing, "He didn't make it!" As firefighters reached the man, the center of the house collapsed and the searing inferno climaxed. As they helped him onto the stretcher, Robert repeated, now to himself, "He didn't make it."

IDLE CAPACITY

FOR ANYONE ALIVE ON JULY 26, 2015, THIS IS NOT FOR YOU. It is a retelling of the singular experience you all shared and will never forget. No, this is for everyone else, so that humanity never forgets an event that was simultaneously both deeply personal and global.

It began at about a quarter to five on that Sunday afternoon, Pacific Time, a day that, up to that point, fit the pattern of thousands of days before and, I suspect, will fit the pattern of thousands more to follow.

We are each the audience of our mind; while we often shape and drive our thinking, we are mainly witness to a chain of thoughts that flow without our volition. The singular experience of that day was the narrative of everyone's passive chain of thoughts.

The narrative was spoken, heard by everyone awake or asleep and in their most familiar language:

"Hello... I hope I am coming through clearly. Sorry to impose, but we have a bit of a situation here," came the voice inside everyone's head.

"I am speaking to you from a spacecraft temporarily parked on the south pole of your moon. My name is Phil, although you will each hear a different, equally familiar name. I represent a civilization many light years away. I have come because we need your help.

"A little background, first. Our civilization is spread across myriad planets in a cluster of stars. We have prospered for eons, but recently made a shocking discovery. You see, our neighborhood is in the path of a giant space-time discontinuity that you call a 'black hole.'

"We've calculated that we have about seven hundred of your years before the first collision. As you can imagine, it's quite a predicament!

"We've been applying the full expertise and computational resources of our civilization to the problem, but we just haven't been up to the task. The best we could do was to predict when the collision would happen and how much more computing power was needed to prevent it. Well, let me tell you, that hardly calmed our nerves—the computing power was astronomical! All seemed lost, but then we managed to come up with a useful suggestion. And that brings us to today's unfortunate interruption.

"The suggestion is a massive computing solution based on, well, a rather *distributed* intelligence. Although our resources have been completely allocated, our sky survey of electromagnetic signals indicated a great source of available capacity here... on Earth!

"We could tell that a reasonably advanced civilization had evolved, obviously capable of transmitting signals over light years to our planet. And we could *also* tell from the *content* of those transmissions, that... and this is a *tad* awkward... well, we could tell that the intelligence was rather underutilized. Put another way, there is a great deal of idle capacity on your planet.

"We truly hate to impose. Really, it's only because we are left with no other choice, but we need that capacity. You won't even notice it's missing! You'll just go about your days in your uninspiring jobs, mindless shopping and eating, following simplistic political bluster, playing video games, and watching reality programming and cat videos, and we will put the rest of your intellectual capacity to work solving our existential problem!

"With the *fabulous* abundance of unutilized intelligence on Earth, it shouldn't take long to puzzle through our dilemma. Your idle capacity will save us! When we have solved the problem, we will let you know. Then we shall be out of your hair, so to speak.

"We will begin immediately. Again, kindly forgive the interruption." With that, the voice ended its speech.

Global reaction was noisy, which was to be expected! NASA's Deep Space Network had managed to isolate the signal during Phil's speech and locate its source in the moon's southern hemisphere. The UN Secretary General scheduled an emergency meeting of the Security Council, but approximately six hours later, before the ambassadors could even change their schedules, Phil's voice returned:

"Brilliant! You are all brilliant! We solved the problem, thanks to you. We never hoped it would happen so quickly. The solution has been checked and re-checked and it is well within the means of our civilization. Have a look at our simulation!"

Those of us who were awake experienced a reverie; those asleep experienced a dream. But we all bore witness to the same spectacle:

An astronomical ball-and-stick cage was assembled around the black hole using giant lengths of diamond spars, thousands of miles thick and millions of miles long, anchored to neutron stars at each vertex. This was done in stages so that the black hole's relentless pull worked against itself and was rigidly resisted by the expanding, yet balanced framework.

First, a cubical cage was assembled from twelve diamond spars and eight neutron stars. Then, more were added. Each star pulled against the black hole, adding resistance against its gravitational tyranny, each carefully selected to oppose a matching counterpart on the opposite side. In this manner, the strain within the cage was kept evenly distributed and, while no match for the black hole, this configuration kept the neutron stars at a safe distance

After the 20th neutron star, the geodesic cage entered realms of strain scarcely found outside of a black hole, and the black hole responded with angry oscillations, as though trying to throw off the gravitational lines that, one by one, sought to pull it apart. But still more neutron stars were placed, another 10, then 20. The black hole vomited great plugs of plasma, surrendering the digested remains of matter long ago consumed. Its oscillations grew more extreme and with each surge came more surrendered matter, the unthinkable undoing of terminal imprisonments of fallen dust, planets, and stars.

Finally, after the 60th neutron star had been placed and carefully counterbalanced, the stellar Buckyball was complete. Radiation shrieked from the black hole and outshone the galaxy. Great plasma jets sprayed erratically, pelting a terrible rain against the neutron stars, causing the cage to spin and shake. The cage joints twisted inside the hammered neutron stars; the diamond spars shuddered but wouldn't yield. The black hole evaporated, its shrieks softening, until, over what may have been 100 years or a microsecond (for space-time was so pinched and twisted there) the black hole gave up its final ghost and was replaced by space picked to complete quantum cleanliness.

"So you see?" Phil exclaimed. "Problem solved! Our engineers are already at work on the design of the neutron star cage. Many thanks again and good-bye! I will leave now and you can go back to sleep or your daily activities. I am sure that *you* can tell the difference."

And most of us did.

THE RECIPE'S PATH

THE SCENT OF MINT-LACED BREAD AWAKENED CARL'S INTEREST in Amanda. It was a cool and breezy late summer day and Carl was walking across campus to his office when the exotic, delicious aroma gusted around him and broke his concentration. The scent was so fresh he knew it had to be from nearby.

He stopped and searched for an open window. Standing between the mathematics and chemistry buildings, he scanned the latter building first, but saw that all of the windows were sealed. Glancing at the mathematics building, he saw a single open window, on the second floor. He decided he could be a little late to work that morning so he proceeded to the window and then paced back and forth, sniffing the air like an Irish Setter to pick up the scent. The tricky breezes caused the scent to dance and tease his nose until he was certain the window was the origin. He went around to the front of the building, entered, and bounded up the marble staircase. Making his way through the corridors, he found the office door that he figured lined up with the window. The nameplate read, "Assoc. Prof. Amanda Coe."

There was a light on inside, and he could hear what sounded like someone rapidly stirring something in a metal bowl. Ordinarily, Carl was not intrusive but this was far too curious a situation for him to ignore. He felt that he looked presentable, even formal, with his briefcase and suit coat and tie. He took a deep breath and knocked. The stirring stopped, and a woman's voice softly said, "Damn it," on the other side of the door. *This may be unpleasant*, thought Carl.

The door opened. As a blast of heavenly mint-laden air wafted past Carl, a young, dark-haired woman looked up at him quizzically and asked, "Yes?" She was attractive and wore casual office attire and a sweater but also a plain white apron, on which she wiped her hands. "Can I help you?" She struck Carl as quite serious, perhaps even cold, but an unannounced visit from a stranger was hardly the time to judge someone's sociability. Or was it?

Carl searched for words. "I am really very sorry to interrupt your work, but I was passing by and I couldn't help but notice the wonderful smell…"

"I hoped leaving the window open would keep the smells out of the hall," she said.

"No, actually I smelled it outside and traced it to this room. I am Carl Rutherford and I work over on the Engineering campus. I do work on digital circuit design algorithms… and related subjects." She showed no interest whatsoever. He added, "If this is a bad time, I…"

She looked at her watch. "I suppose it's OK. I have a few minutes while I wait for some bread to finish baking." She motioned for him to enter but left the door open.

To Carl, entering an office was like entering someone's house. One could learn volumes about a person by studying where they spent their time. Here was a woman who was clearly involved in many endeavors. An impressive computer workstation commanded her desk and was surrounded by a thick flurry of papers. Multiple stacks of books were piled on the floor and tables. The stacks made up tiny libraries on diverse subjects such as graph theory, various cuisines, and psychology, to name a few. There was only a single photograph in the entire office, that of a young man, which was all but obscured by a large bookend. Several documents had large Xs written across them, along with words such as "Crazy," "Wrong!" and lengthier comments written in the same handwriting that he presumed was hers. Scattered about were other artifacts, like a tin of Altoids candies, some small toys, and common office paraphernalia, everything except for a clock (unless it lay buried somewhere). And then there was the small working kitchen, here in the office of a math professor, complete with a refrigerator, sink, stove, oven, and all manner of utensils for food preparation. Several bowls containing remnants of dry ingredients and batter crowded the small countertop. Messy utensils were lying on an adjacent table, placed on magazines to protect the table's wood finish. Then Carl noticed something remarkable about the magazines. Reading around the batter and the implements, he could see Dr. Coe's name on the covers of almost all of them, and a few of the magazines had her photograph. This was clearly an accomplished individual.

She had been quietly observing his concentrated survey, her eyes narrowing slightly. "So, Carl from Engineering, do you make it your business to snoop around offices?" she asked, jolting him out of his thoughts.

Carl cleared his throat, flustered; he found no comfort in Prof. Coe, whose crossed arms and icy expression advertised precious little openness. But rather than apologize again, he decided to plunge ahead, asking, "I don't think I have read about any mathematical research being performed on baking. Is this, well, part of your research?"

"I am deriving a chef," she said matter-of-factly. She gestured to a whiteboard laden with colorful drawings of small circles interconnected with arrows. Scattered about were annotations such as "0.25 c. SC flour" and "2.3 BH eggs." She explained, "You see, from a mathematical point of view, a recipe describes a path through 'recipe space'..."

Carl chuckled; Prof. Coe didn't. Clearly irritated, she said, "You ask a question and then you laugh at my answer. I'm busy. You can laugh your way out the door." She motioned to the door with her hand as she returned to her work.

Carl was dumbfounded by her blunt reply. "I-I'm sorry, and if you want me to leave, I will, but, face it, 'recipe space' has a funny ring to it and when I hear something funny, I laugh." He detected the slightest, most subtle hint of softening in her sober countenance, but she didn't say anything.

He turned to leave, feeling mainly disappointment. *How novel,* he thought, *a highly ambitious and completely self-absorbed intellectual. How very special.*

As he passed through the open door, she called out, "Hey."

Hey? thought Carl. He turned and studied this reflexively guarded woman. She smiled slightly, but only with her shining green eyes. She seemed to want to reach out yet she remained shielded for combat, encased in a protective shell that prevented all but the most equivocal expressions. Hence, "Hey." Carl stood, waiting for more.

She spoke: "I have collected over fifty thousand recipes."

Precious contact had been made, he thought, but he was now late for work. He was dying to look at his watch but if he did he knew the door might slam shut forever, for this was a person who expected rapt attention. But while she intrigued him, he didn't want to become enmeshed with someone who mainly wanted to protect herself or be the center of everything. As this sorted itself out, and he looked at those eyes, Carl smiled, which brought a smile to the professor's entire face.

"What's cooking now?" he asked.

"Oh, that's 77.234.951," she promptly responded. Now he was hooked. He decided he'd be late for work.

"It smells like some very minty sort of bread, if there is such a thing," he said, stepping into the office.

"It's breezy, let me shut the door," she said. As the door shut, Carl felt he had been welcomed at last. He set his briefcase on her desk on a bed of papers. The professor added, "This is a hybrid bread, derived from thousands of recipes." She opened the oven and withdrew a bread pan with a steaming, dark golden loaf.

"It looks splendid!" said Carl. "By the way, do you get many visitors like me?"

She inverted the tin and the bread slid onto a plate. "No," she said, putting the plate by the window. "I guess nobody's curious enough to knock."

He suspected her reputation might also be a factor. "You said the recipe was *derived.* What do you mean?"

She began, "As I started saying before…"

"When I laughed?"

She looked at him and smiled broadly. "Yes, when you laughed. As I was saying, a recipe is a path through 'recipe space,' a space I defined as having six dimensions and, well, we don't have to go into all of that now. But imagine such a space, then a given recipe, be it for bread, ravioli, potatoes au gratin, whatever, is a path through that space. But for it to become a good recipe, say, one that is published, it has to result in something..."

"Tasty!" chimed Carl, "Or else you don't sell many cookbooks!"

"Right," agreed Prof. Coe. "So I am trying to find out what those paths have in common, what the common denominator is of enjoyable food. I am very close to deriving rules that can be used to predict, or synthesize, completely novel recipes. That's my goal: To derive completely new cuisines based on combinations of ingredients nobody would have ever dreamed of, but which we can predict will be delicious." She sliced a piece of bread from the minty loaf and handed it to Carl. He smelled it, smiled approvingly, and took a bite. It was a heavenly mélange of mint counterbalanced with subtle surprising sour notes and a moist richness that was tenderly cut by a tangy aftertaste.

"Oh, this is marvelous," said Carl, still chewing.

"You are eating a bread made with spices from Thailand, roots (pounded, not chopped) of a plant found only in Tierra del Fuego, wheat from the hillsides of the southern Caucuses, eggs from a Blue Heron, milk and butter from Alsacian Jersey cows, and, of course mint, which came from my backyard."

Carl, eating several bites, was overwhelmed. "I have never tasted anything like this. Really, it is so complex, so light, and yet so rich. My mouth, my mouth is blissfully confused. This bread is truly exciting to eat!"

Prof. Coe laughed. "So, it's a keeper?"

"*Yes!* Keep this recipe!" Carl gesticulated and spoke with evangelical zeal, "Build a factory and mass-produce this bread! Hire me as chief of quality control! I'll do it for free!" Prof. Coe laughed so hard she had to sit down. Carl looked at her, engulfed in laughter, and reflected on her initial iciness. He smiled warmly. It had been a long time, he felt, since she had just had fun with someone. This magical person had touched him; he hoped he was touching her.

At that moment, his pocket computer sounded an annoying trill. He yanked it out and stared at the message. "Oh no! I have to interview someone in five minutes! I haven't even looked at her resume! Look, Prof. Coe..."

"Amanda, please call me Amanda."

Carl briefly savored this request but then briskly continued, "Amanda, I will call you later. I would love to talk more about this amazing work you are doing. And I promise not to mention it to a soul. I really have to run. G'bye!" And as Amanda started to wave, he grabbed his briefcase and was out the door as X'd-out papers swirled in his wake.

In the days and weeks that followed, Carl made a point of passing by Amanda's window to try and catch the scent of some never-before-prepared delicacy. He would stop by for a visit, on occasion, being careful not to overstay his welcome. But by October, Carl and Amanda had begun to make room in their lives for each other. Visits were more frequent and were not limited to the office. Discussions no longer centered on Amanda's research or Carl's work travails; rather, new common ground was found and the friendship matured. They cared for each other and started to find tentative, subtle ways to show budding affection.

Carl finally decided that some sort of decisive action was called for. He became inspired to write a valentine, even though it was five months early. It was just a playful poem, but it was a valentine, nonetheless. He put it in a pink envelope, elegantly calligraphed with her name, and planned to surprise her with it the next day over lunch at her office, when they were to try a new meat dish she would derive.

Carl arrived on time, knocked, entered and was immediately overcome by a pungent smell. Amanda, sitting at the computer, quickly looked over but then returned to work, saying only, "One of the recipe algorithms has a bug." The office was filled with a heavy greasy stench that reminded Carl of the time a housemate had fried cheap cat food. The fan over the oven roared and a skillet, encrusted with the failed meat dish, lay submerged in the sink. The window was open and gusts of cold air helped to flush out the foul scent.

Amanda wore a short-sleeved shirt and her arms had goosebumps, so Carl took her sweater off the hook by the door and draped it over her shoulders. He held out the envelope, deciding to take a chance that his out-of-season valentine would interest her more than the problem at hand. "I have a September valentine for you. I was too impatient to wait for the real Valentine's Day... I wrote a little poem." He placed the pink envelope on the desk.

"Not *now*, Carl! Go get some lunch," she said firmly with a dismissive flip of her hand as she focused on the details of a flowchart.

Her words detonated and he instinctively flexed his emotional muscles to brace for the impact. Once again he wondered if he was a blithering idiot for caring so much for someone who could so easily ignore him. He thought that by this time in his life he should be able to trust his instincts. Unfortunately, they were telling him several conflicting things at once.

Suddenly, Amanda gave a long sigh and reached to the back of the workstation and turned it off. She plopped back into her seat. The envelope lay next to the keyboard, unnoticed by her. She looked up at Carl and saw his troubled expression. "Are you OK?" she asked.

He replied, "I have to explain something to you." Amanda, looking a bit weary from her battle with the algorithm, nonetheless paid attention. Then he picked up the envelope and its significance abruptly registered with her. And while she looked with bewilderment, he slid it into his coat pocket. A pink edge was visible. He continued, "I lived in a town which had a 'dog park,' a special fenced in plot of land where dog owners could unleash their pets to run free and frolic with each other."

Amanda listened, even as she looked a bit confused about why he was talking about a dog park.

Carl continued, "My walk to work took me by the park and I'd watch the goings on of dog society as I passed. For the most part, the dogs enjoyed each other immensely. The poor things were clearly starved for doggy interaction and it was fun to see them play chase games or just hang out." He paused, briefly, then took a breath and continued, "But there was one unpleasant activity which really stuck in my mind. That was when an overly amorous dog, a male always, would hound, so to speak, the object of his affection, a completely disinterested and generally irritated female." Amanda was transfixed as Carl's steeled himself to reveal, "I was dating at the time and, well, how can I say this strongly enough, I would rather have been dead than acting out the human equivalent of that hounding."

"Carl, I don't feel that..."

"You just have to understand this about me." His voice was starting to quaver with emotion. "It may sound strange to hear it, but I feel that I am *extremely* human and I feel people are endowed with the ability to decide what they do with their feelings and their impulses. It's our consciences, our minds, our souls, if you will, that are in control, and not some instinctual compulsion." He brought his clenched hands to his chest, saying, with eyes closed, "This is absolutely core to my beliefs." He opened his eyes and locked onto Amanda's as he spoke with a heartfelt fervor, "We aren't some damned marionettes being yanked and tugged by something we do not understand or cannot control. We aren't dogs in the dog park. *We* are in control of *us*. And controlling those impulses makes life a challenge but mastering one's self makes anything possible!"

Tears welled in Amanda's eyes as she looked at the envelope. "Carl, I don't feel you're hounding me. I shouldn't have been so harsh. You deserve better than that."

Carl reached out his hands and she held them as he said, "Life's not perfect. I recently discovered that." They smiled, and Amanda sniffed and wiped a tear from her cheek. He continued, "I can easily understand your need for time. But I need to know you don't see me... as, well, as one of those dogs. I just cannot..."

"Stop it, Carl," she said, squeezing his hands. "I *don't* see you as one of those dogs. I never could. You *are* extremely human and that makes you very special. I am not telling you to go away. I want to see you but sometimes I need to think." She looked at him, then asked, "Will you be giving me the envelope?"

Carl ran his finger along the edge of the envelope. "I suppose I have to think, too," he replied. "Can I help you clean up?"

"No, but thanks," she said, furrowing her brow as she scanned the diagram on her whiteboard. She stood and walked over to the diagram and changed the direction of one of the arrows, speaking softly to herself. Then she stepped back to survey the diagram further.

Carl could see she was going to stay preoccupied. For him to stay and be a distraction would remind him too much of the dogs; to leave would acknowledge Amanda's relative disinterest in him, a realization he was honest enough to admit but which weighed heavily on him. "Well, I'll let you get to your work," he said, turning to leave.

"You can stay, if you want," said Amanda, facing the whiteboard.

"Thanks, but, well… I have some things at the office I need to get caught up on." She didn't respond. He left, reeling from the encounter, and walked home. His suit coat was open to the cold breezes and his tie was blown over his shoulder. The wind caused his eyes to water and he hoped that wouldn't coax him to cry, which he desperately yearned to do, but which he would only dare consider in private solitude.

Once home, Carl turned on a well-selected piece of music, set to repeat indefinitely. He stretched out on his couch, closed his eyes, and thought about how different the man was who brought the envelope to Amanda's office from the one who carried it home. And as he grew intoxicated by the melancholy fourth movement of Tchaikovsky's sixth symphony, Carl tried to relax his defenses to allow himself to cry. But, as always, it was futile.

The afternoon slipped into the graying dusk as the symphony repeatedly descended into its abysmal depths when, through the heavy drone of the cellos, Carl heard the doorbell. He stopped the music then slowly got up, groggy from his inebriation and hunger, shuffled to the door, and opened it. It was Amanda, holding a bag. "Hey," she said, smiling brightly.

For the first time ever, Carl didn't want to see her. *'Hey?'* he thought, *Weren't we beyond that?* He let her in, mainly to stop the cold wind.

Amanda put down the bag, which smelled of heavenly fresh cooking. "I found the bug."

"Uh huh," said Carl, barely masking his consummate disinterest.

She took a deep breath. "It was between my ears… and it misguided my heart. I am so very sorry for ignoring you." Her eyes were more expressive than he'd ever seen them. Gone was the brightness or iciness; instead they were soft and welcoming. "If I ever do that again, you have my permission to throw an eraser at me so I snap out of it. I don't want to lose you." She wrapped her arms around him and held him as tightly as she could, saying, "I don't want to meet at my office anymore. I want to come here, if you'll have me. I want to come here for my escapes, my mini-vacations, my visits to Club Carl."

Carl was being happily pulled from his depths. As seductive as melancholy could be, it was like a narcotic and fooled the senses. Carl greatly preferred joyful sobriety.

"I just have one small request," he said, resting his chin on her head with a sigh.

"Anything," said Amanda.

"Don't stop hugging me," said Carl. His stomach growled loudly in response to the aromas from the bag.

"That will make it hard for us to eat," she said.

This was a real dilemma for him. "OK, first let's eat, and then you can hug me forever."

She gave him an extra squeeze and let go. "OK."

Carl now was fully aware of his dire hunger. "Something smells wonderful!" He rubbed his hands together and looked expectantly at the bag. "Shall we have lunch?"

Amanda took off her coat and carried the bag to the kitchen table. "First," she said, taking out a foil wrapped loaf, "I have your favorite, the mint bread."

"Good old 77.234.951. My favorite!" said Carl.

"Yes, and I also have 243.2.8603.5, which will be our main course." She lifted out a heavy casserole dish encrusted with slices of several kinds of melted cheese, sprinkled on top with some sort of chopped seeds. "This is what I tried to make for lunch today. It is one of the most complicated recipes yet derived and I was very lucky to have almost all of the ingredients in the food locker. I had to have magnolia seeds flown in from central Texas. This is a meat dish with lots of vegetables. It has a type of celery found near West African swamps, which oddly enough has shown up in a *lot* of the derived recipes because it really brings flavors together. The cheeses are from goats from Nepal and Senegal and cows from Uruguay and the Scottish Highlands. There is a variety of vegetables, starting with potatoes and lentils from Ceylon and, oh, a real nice selection of legumes from Southern Europe and the U.S. There was a lot of chopping, frying, basting, you name it. Those are the braised magnolia seeds on the cheese."

Carl was starting to feel weak from hunger. "Wow, you worked hard on this! You can skip explaining the other details for now. I am *dying* to try it. It smells out of this world. By the way, you said it was a meat dish. What's the meat?"

"Ah, yes, there is some wildebeest tenderloin marinated in Korean rice wine." Amanda paused, then said, "And it has just a pinch of, well, I'll say it, little cute red spiders from Indonesia." She saw Carl grimace. "They look just like ants, really!"

"Is that supposed to make them sound palatable?"

"Oh they're quite delicious. I've eaten dozens. They're very sweet and taste like itsy bitsy cinnamon buns."

Carl didn't know if he'd faint from the food or the lack of it. Amanda didn't wait. She heaped a scoop of the steaming casserole on a plate and slid it in front of him, handing him a fork while she opened a bottle of Merlot. After he made a quick scan for spiders, which was negative, Carl took a tentative bite. Flavors exploded in his mouth like the grand finale of the 4th of July. Creamy sweetness intermingled with a complex blend of the succulent wildebeest, accented by the rice wine. The crunchy tasty celery and other vegetables were rounded out by, yes, a perfect counterpoint of cinnamon flavor. He closed his eyes to concentrate on the spectacular culinary composition playing in his mouth. He completed this first bite with a thoughtful sip of the Merlot that was a graceful and fitting denouement. He waited only long enough to say matter-of-factly, "Another keeper," before he enjoyed the next bites, finishing that serving and ultimately helping himself to two more, with a couple refills of his wine. Amanda beamed through this performance of her singular meal, which was rounded out, of course, by slices of mint bread.

Carl was as content as any meal had ever made him. He glowed as he swirled his wine in his glass and smiled with a faraway look in his eyes. "If I gave you a list of ingredients, could your analysis tell me what delicious dishes, if any, could be made from them?"

"Sure," she said, "I'd just have it search recipe space for a solution that would use only those ingredients."

He paused, then spoke, "So, I wonder... What kind of unimaginable delicacy could you create by combining the ingredients from Amanda and Carl?" He knew he was taking a chance asking such a provocative question but, as curator of Club Carl, he wanted to test the limits of their friendship to see if they could be stretched. This was a woman he definitely wanted to see more often, truly, and not because of the food but because of the heart and mind behind it.

The room was silent save the ticking of his watch that now pounded like the Telltale Heart. Amanda looked at the table, then slowly revealed a sweet smile. Carl continued, "What can you do with *my* ingredients, mainly some nuttiness, some warmth, honesty, and a bunch of spices and other tantalizing tidbits I am too shy to name right now. What if you combined those with your ingredients, and you have some spectacular ingredients..."

Amanda waved her hand. "Wait. How can we know what kind of seeds to use for *you*, and what kinds of seeds to use for *me*?"

Carl thought for an instant, then said, "That is a *very* good point. We'll just have to use sweet little seeds for you and big chewy seeds for me!"

Amanda laughed. "OK, that makes sense." She reached out, held his hands and looked into his eyes. "But I don't have to put that into the analysis. I can tell you right now that meal would be supremely delectable, very nutritious and, I assure you, never *ever* filling."

He kissed her hands and said, "Then let's start cooking."

ALFONSE BIKER'S HEAD

ALFONSE BIKER HAD A HEAD FAR TOO LARGE FOR HIS SHOULDERS. He first noticed this excess looking at a group photograph of his high school softball team. To his alarm he saw that, in punctuated contrast to his teammates, his head commanded the small turf of his shoulders. Nobody else had ever commented on this peculiarity. It may have been common politeness that constrained his teammates, his other friends, and his family from commenting on how his upper body was its own caricature, but even the rest of the world had been curiously silent. Alfonse wasn't easily given to paranoid fantasies and he didn't want to start now, but with every glance in a mirror or with every reflection in a storefront window, his eyes stared back from that huge head, hammering home the point: somehow, his deformity wasn't going to be talked about by anyone.

In time, he grew to be preoccupied—not by his awkward skull but about the fuss everyone had been making not to talk about it. He was at odds with himself at how to have respect for these people who were otherwise compassionate, conscientious, and generally quite honest. It was difficult to reconcile their admirable integrity with the conspicuous omission of the subject of his ridiculous head in any communications. In fact, when he thought about their behavior, he grew to be somewhat insulted at first and then, ultimately, disappointed in their whole attitude.

It was childish, he thought, to skirt an issue that was so obviously a significant artifact of their relationships.

Ties of friendship were recognized for what they were. Instead of emotional bonds groomed through shared life experiences, they were mooring lines. They anchored Alfonse to an all-too-common ground with the others. As he cut those lines one-by-one, the tug of freedom grew irresistible as though his head was a great blimp straining to yank Alfonse to lofty intellectual heights.

And as Alfonse Biker became comfortable with his feelings and confident about his conclusions regarding his acquaintances (for they really weren't his friends anymore), he grew haughty and distant, prone to disdain their company and their views on more and more subjects.

Social interactions dwindled to a vanishing few among carefully curated acquaintances, one of whom was named Sylvester.

"Alfonse!" hailed Sylvester one day, hoping feigned enthusiasm would mask the odor of the curdled friendship. "Long time, no see!"

"Indeed", came the severe reply. Somewhere deep within that great head remained a glowing ember of their relationship. It once seemed a bonfire, the brightest of all his former friends, before Sylvester's simplistic greeting erased any remaining doubt: *I was just very close to someone very small*, thought Alfonse.

Sylvester pressed on, half-hearted, with so little left to lose. "So, what have you been up to?"

"You probably wouldn't understand", said Alfonse, shrouded in an air of egocentrism.

Ember snuffed, curdled remains chucked in the garbage, Sylvester yelled through the shroud like a foghorn, "Where did you get such a big head?!"

AMANDA THE PSYCHONAUT

AMANDA QUICKLY PACED BACK AND FORTH IN FRONT OF THE library, carrying her briefcase and staring down at the wet sidewalk, occasionally glancing up to look for Carl's car. Her breath left trails in the brisk night air. The last lights were turned off inside the building and the librarian locked the door as he exited. "Good night," he said to her as he passed, but she didn't notice.

"Eight won't work," she said to herself. She closed her eyes tightly as she plunged into deep thought. "But nine might…"

"Might what?" answered a voice behind her.

"Carl!" She spun toward him. "How long have you been there?" It started to rain and Carl opened his umbrella for them.

"A minute or two," he said, "I didn't want to interrupt the great professor." She flashed a polite smile. "I'm parked over here," he said, "Let's go. It's really starting to come down again." They walked briskly to his car, protected from the cold rain. He opened the door for her, then hurried to the other side and got in, tossing the umbrella into the back seat. He started the car, pulled away from the curb, and accelerated into the traffic.

The inside of the car was warm and comfortable. A late Beethoven string quartet played softly. Amanda closed her eyes, retreating back into her thoughts. Her brow furrowed as she spoke: "I've been thinking about our last discussion." She looked at Carl for a reaction, and got none. She continued, "You know, I'm quite a slave to my obsessions."

Carl remained silent, breathing deeply.

"I truly just want to be Amanda, if I knew who she was."

He looked perplexed. "How could you not know? Everyone else knows. You are one of the most published researchers on this campus. You have a curriculum vitae to die for!"

She was becoming frustrated with him, almost as frustrated as she was with herself. She needed someone to talk to and Carl was one person she always felt she could talk to about anything. "That's a view of *what* I am, not *who* I am," she said with a sigh. Headlights flashed. She continued, stabbing the air, "If I am so damned established why do I dread presenting my work at conferences? I'm mortified up there, but something compels me and I do not want a life of compulsions."

Carl was clearly taken aback, and his own frustration was starting to show. He turned off the music. "Look," he said, "you get up in the morning, you get ready for work, you make a *thousand* decisions throughout the day. That's *you* making the decisions. *You* are the expert on you."

She could feel her stomach knot. These discussions were like dental surgery, in the days before anesthetics. There was never a way of explaining her torment. If she could do that, she would have solved the problem herself. Now, it was just another dreaded rehash of her turmoil. He cared deeply, of course, but he was like a well-intentioned 18th century dentist. She tightened her fists and concentrated on maintaining her composure. She stared straight ahead, saying, "I am not asking anyone else to figure this out but I feel like I am acting in a play, one written by someone who doesn't know me very well or like me very much." She paused, thinking, then said, "I just want to *be*."

Carl was silent, pensive, and kept his eyes forward. Amanda drummed her fingers on her briefcase, counting the seconds to when she would be free from this confinement. The windshield wipers made their squeaky, sloppy syncopation. The car neared her brownstone and Carl steered toward the curb, slowed, and stopped. He twisted to reach in the back seat for the umbrella but not before

Amanda managed a "Thank you" framed by a pained smile. She quickly opened the door, swung herself out, and slammed the door as Carl yelled, "Take a sabbatical! Take a real long trip!"

Amanda stopped and took a breath. She could feel the icy rain starting to soak through her hair, but she didn't want to leave like this. She turned to reply but the car jerked from the curb and pulled away. "I will," she said.

Amanda bounded up the stairs to her home, unlocked the door, entered, and disabled the alarm. She shut and locked the door, stepped into the bathroom, flung her wet coat over the edge of the bathtub, yanked a towel off the rack, and dried off her hair. She realized she was starving, which explained only a tiny part of why she was so upset by the conversation with Carl. She briskly walked to the kitchen, ignoring the blinking answering machine. Her personal and professional life was consumed by a quest for self-knowledge. She grabbed a non-fat raspberry yogurt, a spoon, and a ripe banana.

The challenge of identifying the deepest sense of self had been attempted through the ages with a wide and impressive arsenal. Art, religion, myth, psychotherapy, and mind-altering substances had been used to try to open a clear view of exactly who we are, once all conditioning and pretense had been lifted. She walked out of the kitchen to the end of the hall to a steel door on massive hinges. Each of those strategies had their strengths. She cradled the food in one arm as she tapped a long sequence of numbers into a keypad on the door, after which heavy metal bolts inside the door pulled free and she could swing it open.

But each of those strategies had the same weakness.

She rapidly descended a flight of stairs into a well-illuminated windowless basement as the door closed behind her and the bolts solidly engaged. The quest for the Holy Grail of self-knowledge had always relied on someone's highly subjective interpretation of the evidence. She walked to a workbench stacked high with electronic gear and used her free arm to push clear a space for her meal. She put the food on a table, pulled up a stool, and peeled the banana as she looked across the room and smiled broadly at her spectacular machine. *Now*, she thought, *we'll see direct evidence firsthand.*

The machine, which she had named the Nautilus, after Captain Nemo's submarine, occupied half of the basement and looked like the open cockpit of a small private aircraft surrounded by an impressive wall of computer hardware. The Nautilus applied common principles in a very uncommon manner. As an ultrasound can image the features of a fetus hidden in the womb, the Nautilus could image the structure of the psyche in vivid detail. The visualization showed prominent structures that mapped to major personality traits and minor features that mapped to subtle nuances. And as a spectroscope can use an object's light to reveal its composition, the signals reflected from the structures revealed their psychological content. When this content was combined with the visualization, the result was a vivid worldview of the psyche, a worldview Amanda now planned to explore.

She finished the banana and was too impatient to stay sitting. She ate her yogurt as she walked to the Nautilus, stepping into the cockpit. She flipped a switch on the small instrument panel and waited for a response. A series of buzzes like a telephone busy signal sounded. A dial on the panel pointed to the value eight. She turned it to nine and tried the switch again. A melodic series of tones chimed. "Good," she said. She turned a series of switches as she finished her yogurt, waiting after each switch for the correct tones. After this start sequence completed, she sat in the pilot's seat, slipped on a helmet, and pulled down its visor. Projected onto the visor was a three-dimensional map of her psyche, the surface of which looked like a yellow sphere floating in front of her. She gripped the joystick. "Amanda, the psychonaut," she said to herself, smiling, as she pushed the joystick forward. The image on the visor responded, showing the psyche looming larger and larger ahead of her as she approached its surface.

She began to slowly circumnavigate the surface as she looked for an optimal entrance for her journey. On closer inspection, she saw the surface looked almost lunar with craters and great flat expanses. She could only speculate about the structure of the interior and she imagined that life's experiences ceaselessly piled layer upon layer onto an ever-enlarging surface. The character of this exposed outer layer marked her most recent painful and soothing experiences and doubtless had features from her recent conversation with Carl. But her goal on this trip was to explore deeply buried fundamentals. She wanted to navigate past sedimentary layers of experience and conditioning to her immutable core, the part of her that was "as Amanda as Amanda can be."

As she glided over the surface she saw a looming mountainous structure that resembled a volcano. Here she surmised was vivid evidence of her strongly opinionated temperament, the same temperament that kept her intellect tenaciously focused. She steered the vehicle into the caldera and down a gaping vent. As she descended, she immediately discovered that her psyche was laden with obstacles that blocked her path. She would deftly maneuver around these by magnifying her synthetic worldview and sailing through small fissures. There was a limit to the possible magnification, however, and some of the obstacles were impenetrable. Slowing the vehicle, she parked it next to one of these obstacles, a substantial granite-like boulder. The psychological equivalent of a chemical analysis could be performed on a core sample extracted from an obstacle. In this manner, she could determine, based on the material in the layers, the composition and history of the object. Like the geologic analog, every experience in her life added to the accumulated layers. A routine childhood trip to the grocery store might add the equivalent of a primordial fallen palm frond; a spurned adolescent infatuation, an ancient landslide.

She sliced off a series of layers from the core sample and examined their psychological content. The layers resolved into memories of assorted speaking engagements. Each was laced with inordinate anxiety. Those nearest the surface were recent, consisting mainly of presentations at academic symposia. Deeper in the core sample were speeches in college, then high school. At the end of the sample, pulled from the center of the boulder, was the experience that was the kernel of the obstacle: A humiliating piano recital in 8th grade in front of an unforgiving student assembly. She studied the layers again, reliving the cascade of emotions triggered by that singular 20-minute event from decades ago. A tear rolled down her cheek. She wanted to hug that girl who ran off the stage in the middle of her labored sonata, juvenile catcalls rising in the hall. This had undermined her confidence in front of audiences to this day. She suspected much greater structures lay buried.

She reviewed the global view of her psyche. A twisting red line indicated the path she had taken and her present location. Her destination, the core of the sphere, was distant, particularly if she had to navigate on a minute scale to maneuver around obstacles. There was a considerable cluster of large, dense structures between her and the core and this caused her psychological center of gravity to be far from the core. *If this were a planet,* she thought, *it would wobble.* She wanted to see what had so severely shifted the balance. Cruising toward the center of gravity, she encountered the dense structures. She magnified the worldview to navigate the narrow gaps between these blocks until the gaps disappeared and she was once again forced to stop.

She prepared to take a core sample and began drilling. As her probe drilled deeper, the great depth indicated this obstacle clearly had its origins in her early childhood. She withdrew the core and started the analysis. Due to the density of the specimen, the analysis was painstakingly slow, giving Amanda plenty of time to ponder. When the results were ready at last, she paused before reading the layers. She knew this was going to expose a substantial facet of her personality. She had her suspicions; what she feared was a surprise. She scanned the layers.

At once, a wave of bewilderment washed over her, followed by a sinking realization that she was indeed confronting a fundamental truth about herself. Her eyes watered and the details of the layers were lost in a blur of tears. But what she read she knew was true. With a complex key, she had opened a long-closed vault and the result explained so much to her. In the deepest end of the core, layer after layer showed a little girl, crowded by her four siblings, vying for attention, vying for approval. In layer after compressed layer, her siblings blocked Amanda and put her into the background. Then shallower, more recent layers showed her steeling herself, compelled to overachieve to gain the attention and approval she needed. This came to motivate nearly every decision she made, regardless how minor, for she felt everyone was forever comparing her to her siblings.

So the multitude of layers, even the thinnest ones, were hardened and charged with emotion.

Determination welled up within her and now she was more eager than ever to drive to the center of her psyche. She pulled back on the joystick and steered a course around the enormous obstacles until she found an unblocked path to the core.

As she neared the core, the blocks diminished in size until there were none and she glided through uniform sedimentary layers. These were from the simple, blissful days of her earliest childhood, before peer pressure and innumerable expectations would start relentless lifelong distractions. She felt charged with excitement and she pressed on, descending deeper toward the core. Eventually, even the layering gradually disappeared and Amanda glided into a uniformly illuminated world. She slowed to a stop. She swung to look all around her, trying to discern even the slightest variance, but she could see none. "One hundred percent pure Amanda," she whispered to herself as her heart pounded. Her hands were shaking as she prepared to draw a core sample. The core was easily drawn and as fast as she could enter the commands, it was analyzed. She realized she had been holding her breath and when she saw the results, she exhaled and breathed deeply. "Fantastic," she said. Whereas the other core samples contained highly complex slurries of experience and emotion, this sample contained only two ingredients, both in absolute crystalline purity: Love and curiosity.

Amanda paused, closed her eyes and tried to be touched by these elemental feelings. She could evoke curiosity, of course, but it was immediately tainted by her compulsion to succeed, so that the impulse to discover and invent was supplanted by blind ambition. And with considerable diligence, she could even evoke love; she thought about Carl with much fondness, even possibly love, but her insecurity and lack of self-esteem quickly thwarted this, too. It was all too clear that as long as her center of gravity was far from this ideal center, she could not become "as Amanda as Amanda can be."

Indeed, at first she was surprised not to feel somehow at home here in the center of her soul. But now she realized it had been a very long time since she had been here and she was returning, sadly, almost like a stranger. She slowly sank into melancholy at this thought. What she wouldn't give to grind up the constellation of obstacles and distribute them uniformly, or to even excise them altogether. But what would she then become? Would her mind become as content, and simple, as a child's? Or could she do this and still retain her highly developed faculties? These heroic ideas briefly uplifted her, but the long remarkable day was taking its toll and her nimble mind grew sluggish. She decided it was time to end this first journey. She knew more journeys would follow, and with those would come the answers.

Lifting off the helmet, Amanda turned off the series of switches, and gazed through her surroundings as much as at them. The shutdown sequence completed. She slowly pushed herself from the chair and found her way to the foot of the stairs. The muscles in her back and shoulders were tightly knotted and she stretched toward the ceiling. She glanced at her watch and was startled to see it was nearly 5 am. "Thank God it's Saturday," she said.

She shuffled up the stairs, opened the vault door, and pushed it closed with her foot as she entered the hall. Turning to her bedroom, she closed the blinds and picked up a package of wintergreen mints from her dresser, popping one into her mouth. The room was dark. She looked into the mirror and bit down on the mint. It flashed in her mouth, which made her smile. As she walked to her bed the phone rang. She was curious and found the receiver and picked it up. "Hello?" she asked.

"Are you OK?" came the response.

"Carl, what are you doing up?"

Carl sighed. "I was worried about you. After you got out of the car last night, I was angry and I wanted to put some distance between us." He yawned, then continued, "I drove around for a few minutes and, well, I felt bad about leaving you like that, so I came back but there was no answer at the door. I phoned, but only got your machine. I know you've been working hard lately and I got concerned."

She was touched by his sentiment. "I was in the basement; sorry, but I didn't hear you."

Carl continued, "Look, can we get together later today to talk about last night, and everything else?"

She smiled. "Sure. I will call you."

"Great. I'm going to sleep. I'm exhausted."

"I'm glad you care about me, Carl... and I care about you," Amanda said.

He paused, clearly surprised by her unusual openness. "Thanks," he replied, "I do care." They were silent for a moment then he yawned, saying, "Goodnight."

"Goodnight," she said.

Amanda hung up the phone and lay down on the bed, stretching and relaxing. Too weary to crawl under the covers, she wrapped herself in the bedspread, nestled her head into her cool pillow, and closed her eyes. She immediately slipped into a deep and dreamless sleep, the peaceful sleep of a child, secure in the knowledge she was on her way home at last.

THE GOOD HUMOR MAN

I UNLOCKED THE DOOR, DIDN'T TURN ON THE LIGHTS, FLUNG THE computer bag onto the bed, and then flung myself next to it. The week of meetings had dragged on but was now finally, mercifully, played out. The customer was happy, though they would never admit it. We'd worn each other down, but they had blinked first. Well, another project milestone was crossed off. I'd commuted back to my hotel through an unfamiliar city. Past the Nth hotel lobby, up the Nth elevator, and to the Nth room.

The drapes were open and the cityscape shimmered as tiny lights flickered across vast skyscraper walls in the bronze light of sunset. It was the blissful first minutes in five days when the damned project didn't have to be top-of-mind. One good thing, the one reliably good thing about travelling, was that were still places to discover. I had never been to this city, so I'd decided to stay the weekend. At a certain stage in life, one graduates to freedom, or, rather it is foisted upon you. I was alone now, but decidedly not lonely. I was a free agent; parents departed, divorced from my wife, no kids. Like a cork in the ocean, life's currents took me where they would.

But first, dinner. Actually, first, a scotch and soda. I stood and stretched and walked to the window. The world beckoned; I just needed to change out of my businessman costume. It was a warm spring twilight and I decided to wear my alma mater T-shirt in case

I ran into fellow alumni. Anything to improve the odds. Amber streetlights blinked on and, looking down at street level, I noticed a boxy white truck parked across the street. Its glossy finish reflected the yellow streetlight under the darkening sky. Even from this distance I could read the foot-tall words, in a bold chocolate-colored font: "Good Humor." With its rounded corners and edges, it could have just cruised in from my past. I hadn't seen a Good Humor ice cream truck since I was a kid and one parked by my junior high school, across from the school exit. What brilliance. That Good Humor Man had the school well trained, for we lined up daily. He was probably on his private island right now, living large on an annuity of misspent lunch money.

Maybe I could get an ice cream bar before that scotch. What a perfectly compulsive thing for a free man to do! I changed my clothes, grabbed my wallet and cash, and headed out.

As I neared the truck I could see it was festooned with familiar illustrations of ice cream bars, rockets, sandwiches, and cones. From behind the truck walked the Good Humor Man, who must have heard my footsteps. He smiled broadly, fitting the part to a T. But he had clearly been around the block many times, in every respect, for under his Good Humor cap was a shock of salt and pepper hair, uncombed perhaps since it was last washed. A weathered, unshaven face was illuminated by shiny blue eyes and a warm smile of neglected teeth.

I rounded the truck to the business side on the curb and asked, "Do you have ice cream bars with the chocolate candy in the middle?"

"Sure do!" came the snappy reply. His arm disappeared deep into the freezer. He rooted around among an unseen icy smorgasbord and pulled out an ice cream bar, *the* ice cream bar, like a magician pulling a rabbit out of a hat. Handing it to me, he noticed my shirt with its stitched alma mater logo. "You a scientist at the university?" he asked.

"No, I just have a degree from there," I replied, handing him the cash.

"What in?" he asked, taking the money.

"Aerospace," I said.

That lit a fuse. The Good Humor Man continued, as he handed me a napkin and processed my $2, "Because I wrote a story

explaining time travel, forward and backward. I sent it to Nassau."
NASA, I thought, but didn't want to derail the spirited monologue.
He continued, putting away the bills, "... and I asked if they could
turn my story into equations. They wrote me back and said that
nobody could turn my story into equations." Then, turning to me for
emphasis, his face stern, he added, "That's how advanced the theory
was."

I unwrapped the ice cream bar, "I see," and took a bite.

The Good Humor Man scratched his grizzled and stubbled chin.
"But a college educated fella like you, they'd listen to you. Maybe *you*
could help turn my story into equations."

I wanted to throw a wet blanket on this, one that was thick,
dripping wet, and heavy. "Sorry, pal. You'll have to ask someone else.
I have to get going."

As I started to turn his eyes widened. "Wait!" he exclaimed,
grabbing my arm. I shook free, then he relaxed and his easy smile
returned. "Sorry... got carried away." He seemed sincerely contrite.
This odd but Good Humor Man was scrawny and harmless, so I
stayed put. There was no point in being huffy; after all, I was Mr.
Independent Man About Town. Also, last I checked, my social
calendar was wide open.

As he studied me, he said, "Ya know what, friend? You look
familiar."

Between bites, I replied, "I don't think we've met," as that was
kinder than saying, *No way would I forget a nut job like you*, although
I'm not sure he deserved the kindness.

He seemed intent to make a point. He studied me for a second
and cocked his head. His bony hand unlatched the freezer door and
swung it open. He reached back into the freezer. His face puzzled,
then brightened as he exclaimed, "Sure, we've met!" and pulled out
a school binder dusted with frost. He tapped the binder against the
truck to knock loose the crystals and handed it to me, laughing as
he said, "You've probably been looking for this!"

I held the binder in my hand and tried not to cough. He laughed
at my reaction. How could I be holding a binder from my time in
junior high school, with my name written in my handwriting and
decorated with my doodles? I tossed the remains of the ice cream bar

and opened the binder, to his giggling. With each page that I flipped, I was shocked to see my notes.

"How?!" I blurted, staring at him incredulously.

With an easy grin, he slowly swept his hand to the right and then to the left: "Forward and backward." He held up a finger for me to wait while he reached back into that incredible freezer. Or was it he who was incredible? What was happening? I frantically looked around and felt a small measure of comfort to see the same buildings around me, stars still in the sky that still contained the single moon.

From the freezer, he retrieved a small icy chunk of something flat and brown. He seemed surprised by the ice. He carefully flexed the block until the ice broke away. It was a wallet. Handing it to me, he said, "That was way in the back, in the desk drawer in your bedroom… in the house on MacArthur Drive."

I tucked the binder under my arm. Fingers trembling now, I had to concentrate to hold the wallet that crackled as I slowly opened it. Whether due to the coldness of the object or my insensibility, my fingertips felt numb as I clumsily peeled open flaps that had been long closed. Peering in, I could see my school ID, with its happy pubescent photo, and the little inspirational notes I'd once stowed to help me brave the uncharted passages of early adolescence.

Gesturing to the freezer with his thumb, he said, "It's all in here, buddy," tapping the truck for emphasis.

My heart in my throat, I fixed my gaze on this strange man who had violated my history. He had rifled through my memories like they were packages of ice cream in his truck. A sense of dread and utter powerlessness began to wash over me. Sensing this, he softened and put his cold hands gently on my shoulders as he spoke, "Man, don't worry, man. I thought you'd be happy. These are gifts I am giving you."

I stepped toward the freezer door and peered in as he stepped aside, chuckling. "Go ahead!" The dark interior admitted only scattered yellow streetlight. Steam from the dry ice obscured wrapped ice cream bars and other Good Humor fare packed in cardboard boxes stenciled with serial numbers and product names. He spoke again: "You just have to know where to look."

I realized that I was catching my breath; my chest heaved as my syncopated heart raced. I wanted to run, but I stared again at my treasures. I saw them as props, fabricated by the Good Humor Man's unfathomable alchemy. They couldn't be the real artifacts. "This is too much," I said, turning to walk away.

"Them's the last treats for you if you leave now." I kept walking as he raised his voice, "No letters from Sarah! None of them Christmas toys you remember!"

I quickened my pace and crossed the street toward the hotel. "No mother! No father!" he yelled.

I froze in my tracks and stared at him. His amiable face now flexed and hardened as he delivered a command, "Help turn my story into equations."

I marched over to a trashcan, lifted the lid and heaved in the notebook and wallet, shouting, "That's what I think of your treats… and your story!"

As I turned to see his reaction, my eyes and my brain couldn't agree on what they saw: The truck was gone, without a sound, without a breeze.

I looked in the trashcan: No notebook or wallet.

I stood still to wait for my breathing to gradually ease. My wits reassembled, piece by piece, like the slow motion rewind of a shattering vase. The sound of traffic seeped back into my consciousness and I gazed skyward to confirm the cityscape, the stars, and the moon.

Secure in my sanity, I nonetheless wrestled to square the episode with reality. I was oblivious to hurried pedestrians that brushed past as I stood by the trashcan. Had too much hard work caused my psyche to unravel? Or was the Good Humor Man a twisted angel sent to compel me to drop anchor to my past, lest I drift away?

I returned to the hotel and made my way to the restaurant. I enjoyed that scotch, then another, as I dined at a window seat with a view of the street. I tried to shake it off, but I still glanced outside between sips, between bites. The truck never returned that night or ever since.

Over the days and weeks after that trip, my future resumed its drift like that cork on the ocean. I wouldn't have it any other way. I rather prefer for the past to stay in the past, regardless of the magic of the Good Humor Man.

THE FUTURE DOORKNOB

IT WAS A LAZY AUTUMN SUNDAY AFTERNOON. THE SUN SLANTED through the blinds and painted warm tracks across the living room of Amanda and Carl's house. For Amanda, it was a welcome break from a relentless frenzy of research she had been conducting both on her computer at home and at the university. Carl could tell she had accomplished something that pleased her and he knew she'd tell him about it soon, when it suited her. He could see from her dreaminess that she was savoring something splendid.

They sat snuggled next to each other on the couch, watching dust motes float through the beams of light as chamber music softly played. Amanda sighed and then she lazily lifted her arm and pointed at the front door. "Look at that doorknob," she said. The door had a utilitarian and undistinguished bronze-plated doorknob. A cluster of newspaper rubber bands ringed its grimy, narrow neck. Amanda asked, "Why is the doorknob *that* color and not some other color? Why is it made of *those* materials and not some others? Why does it have *that* shape?"

The time had just arrived, thought Carl, when he'd learn of her accomplishment.

They studied the doorknob for a second before she continued, "I don't think we really can know exactly what that doorknob *is* because we don't know what it *isn't*. And what if that doorknob appeared on a Mayan altar a thousand years ago? It would have been received as a gift from the gods. A thousand years from now, it may be some peculiar metal plug from a forgotten era."

Carl stared at the doorknob as if it had fallen out of a flying saucer.

Amanda continued, "And everything is like that doorknob, Carl. *Everything.*"

Carl walked over to the doorknob. He glided a finger along its contours, catching the rubber bands and giving them a tug. He crouched down and tried to see his reflection in its blunt surface but it had been scuffed by countless scratchy mittens, bejeweled fingers, and collisions with the wall, such as when the doorstop had broken. Still, the simple, beaten fixture now possessed an aura of mystique. Amanda smiled as she gazed at Carl's exploration. To Carl, the doorknob now had an almost electric charge. He then studied the molding around the door and followed a hairline crack from a corner of the door along the wall to the ceiling. The electricity followed his gaze and as his eyes swept the room the commonplace became almost overwhelming. He went back and sat next to Amanda and as he quietly scanned the room, she leaned her head on his shoulder.

"Knowing what something is, or isn't, is just a first step," Amanda said. "Knowing what it was and will be completes the picture." He nodded as she continued, "I've been studying plant and animal evolution, studying it a *lot*." She started to gesture as she always did when she was getting revved up with an idea, and she had Carl's rapt attention. "Even though life has evolved in fits and starts, there has always been a continuity. From the Cambrian Explosion to—"

"The what?" asked Carl.

"Oh, the Cambrian Explosion was when the first complex animals appeared, about 600 million years ago. Because there was no competition, there was a mind-boggling variety of animals. There were several basic body plans from that era that have never existed since. Very strange animals that flourished for millions of years but which don't look remotely like anything alive today. As I was saying, there is a continuity even from those bizarre creatures to us."

"But that's Evolution 101, right?" said Carl.

"Right," said Amanda, "But I discovered something new which underlies it all." She took a breath and sat up as her eyes began to gleam. "I discovered—follow me here—that for the evolution of living things, when you model with the right parameters, the change of the change of the change of the change is almost constant; it falls within a very narrow band of randomness. Give me a starting point, then, with high confidence, I can roll back time to see what an animal evolved from and I can roll it forward to see what it will evolve into."

Carl was fascinated and Amanda took his hand. "Come here," she said as she quickly led him to her computer. She sat at the desk and tapped a few commands. An image of a small prehistoric bird appeared.

"Look at that," she said.

"It's a feathered lizard," said Carl.

"It's one of the earliest ancestors of birds. Now watch," said Amanda, "I will show how this bird's evolution progressed." She tapped in commands that started a numeric counter labeled "generations" to increment at a furious pace.

Carl watched for a minute. "But it isn't changing," he said.

"Keep watching," said Amanda. The animal remained virtually intact, except that its legs and neck slowly tapered until, almost in the blink of an eye, it transformed in a spasm of development into a creature resembling a modern wren.

"Wow!" said Carl. "Is that what really happened?"

"What you just saw," said Amanda, "was my model of the evolution superimposed over a sequence reconstructed from the actual record."

"It's an almost perfect match!" said Carl.

"Remember the narrow band of random change I mentioned?" Carl nodded as she continued, "If I run the simulation again, the randomness alters the outcome but the result will still be a wren, just one with slightly different proportions and coloring." She proceeded to rerun the simulation, which yielded the wren variation. "And I have run the test for hundreds of insects, plants, fish, and even hominids.

I had to sort out some initial kinks, but since then it has worked beautifully every time."

"That's incredible!" shouted Carl as he wrapped his arms around her. "How about if you roll it forward? What will this cute little bird's descendants look like?"

"This guy stays the same for a helluva long time. But you should see what happens to spiders. It'll give you nightmares."

Carl shuddered at that. "I'll pass. Amanda, this is one of your greatest triumphs!" He kissed the top of her head.

Amanda swiveled around and looked up. "Thank you," she said with a polite smile. Then she brightened up again, saying, "I am even *more* excited about how I want to use it next!"

"To study the evolution of Republicans?" asked Carl.

Amanda smirked, then quickly became focused and serious. She began, "Inventions and technology evolved through history, subject to forces analogous to those in natural evolution." She started to gesture again and Carl was completely absorbed. "I believe," she said, "that the same deeply buried rules of natural evolution also can describe the evolution of inventions, machines, anything."

"Meaning that you can roll backward and roll forward the evolution of any man-made object?"

Amanda smiled proudly and nodded.

Carl continued, "Of doorknobs? Cobblestones? Hamburgers?"

Amanda, caught a bit off guard by his selection, paused, then replied, "Well, yes."

Carl frowned a little, uncertain, but decided it was unwise to probe. "That's great," he said, somewhat forced.

Amanda was undeterred: "I want to apply the rules to something to prove my point. You'll see. I'd like to try it on..."

"How about the doorknob?" asked Carl.

She pondered this for a moment, then shrugged. "Why not?"

Amanda picked up a screwdriver, carried it to the doorknob, and started to unscrew it. "I just need to record it to get started. I'll put it back when I'm done," she said.

"Need any help?" asked Carl.

Amanda was already removing the second screw. She shook her head so Carl decided to stretch out on the couch. He grabbed the newspaper from the coffee table and opened to the movie reviews. He put on headphones and listened to the Lt. Kijé Suite while reading entertaining reviews of poorly rated movies.

Amanda buried herself in the task at hand: recording and encoding the doorknob for the evolution visualization. After about an hour, the capture was complete. She put the doorknob back on the door, quickly screwing it in place.

"I am now ready to visualize the evolution of the doorknob," she confidently announced. Carl's headphones made him oblivious and he blissfully hummed and smiled. Amanda decided not to disturb his contentment.

Sitting back at the computer, Amanda displayed the doorknob as it appeared in its current incarnation. "Now, what are you going to become?" she asked, smiling to herself as she tapped in commands to roll the doorknob forward through its evolution. As "generations" raced by, spiral grooves appeared in the face of the doorknob. The grooves slowly deepened until the doorknob resembled a nautilus.

"What?" Her eyebrows furrowed. "That's ridiculous!"

She ran the simulation again. This time the doorknob morphed into a sphere wrapped in a spiral of large beads. Puzzled, she rechecked the inputs, and then once again simulated the doorknob's future evolution. This time the result looked like a snowflake. Again and again she ran the analysis and the doorknob evolved. Each iteration was peculiar and unique, an almost psychedelic variety of fantastic predictions.

Carl, still oblivious, sporadically giggled at the movie reviews in the background.

Speaking to the doorknob, Amanda asked, "OK, then what about your past? Where did you come from?" She tapped in commands to roll the doorknob back through its evolution. The doorknob slowly elongated into a cone with spiral grooves. It stretched longer and longer through successively earlier generations. "What in the world is that?" she asked aloud. She ran the reverse evolution simulation again; a twisted toroidal shape resulted.

Sitting back in the chair, she stared quizzically at the strange image for several minutes. Then she closed her eyes and massaged her temples, searching deep into her expansive mind for a plausible theory for the bizarre results. "What's going on?" she repeatedly whispered to herself, mantra-like, as she massaged harder.

Amanda rebooted the machine and ran the bird evolution again. It exactly followed the historic record, yielding another wren variation. Then she loaded the doorknob recording. She paused, exhaled in exasperation, and started the reverse evolution, saying, "Come on, let's keep it sane." Her face cringed as she saw tentacles expand and curl from a central shaft. She meticulously double-checked the recording of the doorknob, the rules that controlled the evolution, and the random input. All looked perfect.

By now Carl had stopped his reading and stood behind her, looking at the tentacled creation. He asked, chuckling, "So is that what a Neanderthal doorknob looked like?" Amanda shot back an icy glare that froze Carl to the core. "Just asking!" he responded, "But isn't that what you think you're looking at?"

Amanda studied the evolution replay, ignoring Carl. He patiently waited for a verbal reply but after he realized it was not pending, he grew rather irritated with her demeanor. Had this occurred earlier in their relationship, he would have forced the issue, which would have precipitated a messy argument. Carl had extremely little tolerance for being ignored, but his time with Amanda had taught him important things about her. First, Amanda loved him, and that made it possible to excuse practically anything, except, perhaps, being ignored. But second, she was a woman of almost unequalled intensity and focus, and Carl found that absolutely irresistible and had cultivated deep respect for her. Reviewing these facts, Carl calmed down and decided it was best to leave Amanda to her work. It was late.

He placed his hands on her shoulders and kissed the top of her head. "Goodnight," he said, but now Amanda was consumed in thought.

Carl awoke the next morning to a clanging, crashing sound from the living room. He sprang out of bed and ran into the room, where he saw the metal wastebasket rolling in the middle of the room, trash scattered across the floor. Amanda was rubbing the toes of her shoe, cursing to herself. She looked pale and totally spent. She slumped in her chair, resting her weary head on her hand and her eyes on the screen that Carl could not see, but which he could imagine. He had never seen her in such a state. She didn't even notice him standing there. The room was chilly and Carl started to shiver so he quickly slipped on his clothes and then hurried to her.

On the screen was a tree-like structure, yet another bizarre doorknob incarnation. She buried her head in her hands. "I am *never* going to succeed at this." Carl could see that her eyes were still open, staring at something that wasn't there. He could say so many things, but he knew her feelings had to come out. She continued, shaking her head, "I am so tired of being so stupid, so horrible, so very awful." She clenched her hair and pulled.

Carl grabbed her hands and exclaimed, "Amanda, don't go there! Don't let this thing take over."

"But I almost have it working. I know I can get it to work!"

"Listen to me: Nothing, *nothing* is worth your sanity!"

"I can't even cry about this," she said, looking up, her face strained with frustration. "Something inside of me says if I cry it will weaken my resolve, that I will fail for sure." She took a deep breath. "God, I hate being me!" She clenched her fists and then fixed her eyes toward the front door at the cheap brass-plated orb that possessed her.

"Look at me!" said Carl, standing as he let go of her. She turned to him. "The goal was there before you were obsessed by it; it will still be there after you escape from this frustration. You've been working madly for weeks. You have to decompress! You can come back to this!"

"Great. Come back and be an idiot and fail," she said, head in her hands again, this time with her eyes closed. Carl gently held her wrists and moved them from her head. She relaxed her fingers and let her hair slide between them.

Carl's hands glided into hers and she looked up at him as he said, "It is so easy for me, on the sidelines, to say it will all work out. It is so damned easy for me, who hasn't fought this thing, to tell you how smart and capable you are and that you will succeed. That type of talk is cheap and I won't give you cheap talk."

"Look," he continued, "I have had the advantage of a good night's sleep, but you're firing on one, maybe two cylinders."

"Don't tell me I need sleep," she warned, pulling back her hands. She sat and stared at the floor as she rubbed her temples again.

"I'm not. But I have been thinking about your theory and, well, hear me out." He paused for acknowledgement but didn't receive any. She was brittle, so he delivered his next words like tentative steps on uncertain ice. "The way I see it, the wren is the result of natural influences. Natural influences can be independently measured… and they are the same for all time." Her face was buried in her hands. He pressed on: "The doorknob? C'mon! People designed that, people acting on ideas that popped into their heads. Every day, people dream up stuff that nature never would *or ever could*. It's why one doesn't find a Saturn V growing in the forest."

After a pause, she looked up with a smile. Her green eyes were reddened by tears and lack of sleep. She sniffed. "It would be cool, though, wouldn't it?" she asked, wiping away tears.

Carl turned quizzical. "To find a forest of Saturn V rockets?"

She burst into laughter, "No, you idiot! To predict what inventions will become!"

The ice was firm. He briefly joined the laughter, but then added, "I don't think so. It would mean that everything that makes people, well, capable of thought and creativity, all of that would be essentially algorithmic and predictable."

She pondered this, as he added, "You and I, what we will become… is that something you think can be predicted? Would you want it to be?"

Amanda stood, wrapped her arms around Carl, and warmly kissed him. "I think I already know."

He got a devilish look in his eyes as he quickly leaned over and scooped her up in his arms and began to march toward the front door.

Amanda laughed heartily, asking, "Where are we going?"

Gesturing at the door, he answered, "Out!"

He swiveled for her to reach the famous doorknob, which she turned and then pulled the door open. He stepped through the door and said, "Now close it."

"But it's locked and I don't have the key!" she said.

"Perfect!" he said. Amanda hesitated, so Carl quickly reached for the doorknob and pulled it shut.

"Carl!" she yelled.

He lowered her to the porch and sat beside her. Sunrise was beginning to whitewash the sky.

"We're going to walk to town to get away from *that*," he said jerking his thumb over his shoulder at the doorknob. She had closed her eyes, though she was still awake, and leaned against him.

He continued, "Then, after we grab coffee and a bite, we will... *call a locksmith!*"

"Brilliant," she deadpanned.

They began their walk downtown and the world slowly awoke around them.

LETTER TO THE LADY

April 30, 1839
Dear Lady Impene,

Please excuse my penmanship. I am struggling as best I can with my arm in a cast and the cast in a harness. As you may have guessed, the experiment wasn't a resounding success. The mud sea is still unconquered. But, the experiment wasn't a resounding failure, either. After all, I am living proof of that. I'm confident that with some additional support from you, the objective will be had. I'm bursting at the seams to report what happened!

I arrived at the jump-off point at dawn. As usual, the sky was densely overcast. The mud below was as thick, stagnant, and revolting as ever. I unpacked the balloon and proceeded to inflate it by blowing into the mouthpiece. I was well rested and well fed. I figured I could inflate it in six hours. In fact, it took me only five. The new wool composite insulation was living up to all expectations: The balloon retained my breath's heat well and tugged my arms upward. I was certain I'd soon be gliding cleanly over the rancid mire. I was certain the unwalkable and unsailable mud sea would be conquered forever.

I held my breath and leapt off the cliff, grasping the balloon tightly with both hands. A draft of wind blew down the cliff, caught the balloon, and buffeted it about, slamming me against the cliff, resulting in my arm injury. When the brief gust subsided, though, my true fate became apparent. I was sinking agonizingly toward the mire. Immediately, I unpinched the hose leading to the mouthpiece and blew furiously, but each breath I injected invariably cost at least as much warm air that leaked out in the process.

My toes touched the mud, which was rather cold and uninviting. I was certain I'd never live to tell this tale and that the revolting goopy sea would claim another fool. But when I had sunk to my ankles, my fall stopped. The lift in the balloon had stalled my descent with the minute assistance of my feet against the mud. Still holding the blow hose tightly with my good arm, I decided I couldn't last walking across the sea, so I made my way back to the cliff.

With the lifting assistance of the balloon, I managed to climb back up the cliff, clinging tightly to it when the gusts threatened to toss me back. I made my way back to the village unassisted and feel more anxious than ever to try again to transit the mud.

Lady Impene, while I was too heavy to fly, I was also too light to sink. And while my performance was inelegant at best, allow me to remind you that the first time an attempt is made at anything, we are always an amateur.

Sincerely, and with highest regard,
Your humble servant,
Erasmus Dinker

THE DEVOLUTION
OF ALEX

"RUTH, ALEX DOESN'T FEEL LIKE PAINTING ANYMORE," REPORTED Guido. "He's taken to finding large trees and curling up on the grass in the shade. He sleeps now."

"He sleeps?!" responded Ruth from behind her easel.

"Like a baby," said Guido. "And yesterday he said he didn't care if he was ever creative again. He said he was going to stop being, well, one of *us*."

"What does he hope to do? What does he want to become? How can he become anything if he sleeps and isn't creative?" Ruth was clearly concerned and had risen from her easel. "Where is he now?"

"I saw him at the park this morning. He said he was trying to devolve into a lesser life form that didn't know about things like art or creativity. He hopes to be a slug by next week."

"Guido, take me to him. Take me to Alex," demanded Ruth. They left the building and proceeded dutifully to the park. When they arrived, Guido pointed to a figure lying motionless under the lush boughs of a massive oak tree.

"That's him," he said. Their pace quickened. Ruth, unable to hold back her contempt any longer, yelled, "Alex! You have no excuse to be out here!" She continued marching while regaining her breath. "Do you hear me? Wake up! Get up and get into the world and create, man!"

Alex didn't respond to her commands. When Ruth and Guido arrived at the tree, he opened his eyes.

"Look at me," said Ruth.

"Look at her," said Guido.

Alex looked in the direction his head was facing, which was toward Ruth's ankles. Ruth got on her hands and knees, straining to make eye contact with him. "Alex," she said, straining also to be diplomatic and collected, "You were—*are*—a fine artist. You're productive, creative, and an inspiration to us." She immediately regretted using her finest compliments so soon in the appeal. Alex was unmoved. Ruth continued, "You know, there's nothing wrong, nothing unusual in the least with having a mental block. Is that your problem? Are you just, well, burnt out?" He stared. "It'll pass," she said tenderly.

Alex spoke. "In the bottom right hand drawer of the old sewing table in the closet in my studio are some paint brushes. I forgot about them when I was throwing away all of my supplies. Will you throw them away for me?"

Ruth instantly stood up, pressing her hand to her lower back. "All right! I don't care if you ever create again! And I don't care if you become a snail by next week!"

"A slug," inserted Guido.

Ruth and Guido turned briskly and began to walk away. Then Ruth stopped, looked back, and yelled, "Alex, for all I care, you can just lie out here and become whatever you want!"

And he did.

CARL'S LEAP

As he waited for Amanda in the crowded coffee shop, Carl steeped in the din of animated conversation and grinding coffee. Music of an indiscernible genre was all but lost in the cacophony. The gentle downward breeze from the ceiling fans delivered steady aromas of roasted coffee beans intermingled with the heavenly scent of freshly baked pastries.

The ambience induced a fanciful reverie about the singular woman he awaited. He considered their careers, trajectories begun nearly simultaneously but which then followed vastly different altitudes and ranges.

Amanda soaked up the spotlight shown on her academic accomplishments. She flourished in it like a spiny cactus, thought Carl, before catching himself: *That's unfair*. She was a glorious tropical bloom, he decided, thriving, as only she knew how. But he was in the shade, a mushroom or some strange fungus tucked in the undergrowth and seen only by those with peculiar predispositions.

Amanda earned many accolades, surely with tenure right around the corner. If this were a drag race, Amanda's car would be vanishing ahead while he fumbled with initial gear changes. *But it's not a race*, he'd tell himself… again and again. Maybe Amanda was a drag racer and he was an off-road racer. He tried that on for size. Sure! They'd both win, but different races. Alas, Carl couldn't fool himself for long. With a casual pivot of her formidable mind, he knew Amanda could master off-road racing. Then he would see her car disappear in a plume of dust and dirt.

He needed something unassailable, despite his near idolization of Amanda. At last inspiration struck; he managed to cut the Gordian knot when, as if on cue, Amanda breezed into the shop. She acknowledged Carl with her warm smile and threaded her way through the congestion, while Carl girded himself to share the news.

He stood and they embraced. After a moment of small talk, they followed coffee shop protocol to order lattes and ponder whether to order the eclairs with the dark chocolate icing.

After a caffeinated exchange of esoterica, their conversation reached the lull that Carl had been waiting for. He took a deep breath and made direct eye contact with Amanda. He was about to say something, which, if not taken in the intended liberal spirit, would make him sound like a blithering idiot. What moments ago seemed decisive and unassailable now felt like an act of desperation to salvage his assaulted ego; moreover, this act required the full faith of the very person he sought to impress. As far as he was concerned, he was about to leap off of the lofty bridge of their relationship with a bungee cord of trust wrapped around his ankles. He wanted to be sure it wouldn't be a one-way trip. Amanda was characteristically sober and receptive. The moment had come; he felt safe and put his trust in the bungee cord.

He cleared his throat, leaned forward, and spoke earnestly: "I think it is entirely possible... that some day I could become the Queen of England."

Amanda laughed uproariously.

Amanda one, Carl zero, he thought, *but this isn't over yet.*

Several patrons turned to look and Carl forced a smile to suggest he had just told a joke. It worked and people soon lost interest.

Carl sighed and waited patiently for Amanda's laughter to die down, but it didn't. "I don't think you understand," he said. The bungee cord wasn't feeling tight yet.

Amanda paused in her laughter just short of soiling herself and said, "What's not to understand about becoming the Queen of England? Seems pretty clear to me." She then resumed her unwelcome reaction to Carl's idea.

Over this, Carl continued, "What I'm trying to say is that we can become anything we want. To make that point as vivid as possible, I picked someone as different from me as I can imagine. But I will say this: I am referring to a current Queen of England; I am not proposing time travel."

"Well that certainly anchors the idea in bedrock," she replied, over only occasional eruptions.

Carl persevered, deciding his leap might end in a watery splash and he'd have to tediously climb back to the bridge to regain Amanda's respect. "What I'm trying to do is force us to define the boundaries we set for ourselves. You appear to find it ridiculous to consider me as a possible Queen of England." He didn't wait for a reaction. "OK, how about if I said it's possible that I could become an accountant some day, remaining a man? Do you have a problem with that?"

She was smiling now, working the issue as she wiped away the last tears. "No," she said.

"So," said Carl, "somewhere between a man who is an accountant and the Queen of England is the boundary of a box you'd implicitly have me inhabit."

"Well…"

Carl continued, "No, we are talking about the universe of Carl. The exhaustive universe of all possibilities, as long as we obey the laws of physics."

"But be realistic, Carl. What chain of events would have to happen for you to be crowned Queen of England? Seems like a pretty long list."

"And?"

"And maybe there are other laws to consider that put limits on these possibilities. Why not say you'll be the Queen of England and also live in a cave on Pluto?"

"Why not?" said Carl. "Really, tell me why that could never ever happen."

"I can't, just like I can't say you couldn't win the lottery ten times in a row." She continued, "But statistically speaking, the odds of that happening are so infinitesimal as to make it effectively impossible, from any meaningful point of view."

"I can grant you that, but the lottery isn't won by human will or imagination. It's purely chance. What I claim is that human potential is far, far more limited by spirit than physics or math." Now Amanda was smiling with him, rather than at him. Carl was back on the bridge.

But Amanda wanted to continue exploring this idea. She was never one to sign on the dotted line without reading all of the fine print. "What if two people want to be queen? What if they wanted to live in the same cave?" she said.

Carl waved his hands. "That's pointless devil's advocacy; a mind game."

"And saying you could be the Queen of England in a cave on Pluto isn't a mind game?" she retorted. She retained a half smile but Carl was chafing at this examination. His eyes grew fiery.

"Playing with possibilities is not a mind game!" he exclaimed. Again, heads turned but he didn't care. He felt he had opened his soul to Amanda and she had laid it on an operating table.

"Then what kind of game are you playing when you play with possibilities?" she said.

"The only game worth playing," he replied. "The alternative is to accept one's lot in life. Born a peasant, stay a peasant." Carl could feel emotion welling up inside him, but he caught himself before becoming angry again. "Look, this is too close to home for me to see you clinically dissect it."

"Carl, I..."

"No, I just need to take a break from this. I want to talk about it with you, but I am not ready now. I just want to walk home. I'll call you later. It's OK, really."

Amanda was empathetic but clearly disappointed. "Are you sure?" she asked.

Carl nodded. He got up, kissed her forehead, and left the coffee shop.

After the several block walk, he turned up the stone path to his front door. The walk calmed him, as walks always did. He noticed a white piece of paper that had blown onto the porch. Picking it up, he saw it was an advertisement for a local car wash. An automobile, standing on its rear tires and grinning from headlight to headlight, cheerily proclaimed the offer in bold red letters against white glossy card stock.

He unlocked his door and proceeded to the wastebasket when he noticed a tiny black spot, barely perceptible, on the white field of the card. It caught his eye for no particular reason, except that it was the only flaw in the simple card. Carl stopped and wondered, hardly giving it half a thought, but then it grew into a full thought that quickly matured into curiosity.

He turned from the wastebasket and walked to his office. From the bookshelf he pulled down the old high school lab microscope he had owned for years but seldom used. He set it on his desk and slid the card under the lens. Turning on a reading lamp, he twisted the neck of the lamp to shine on the specimen, and peered into the eyepiece. He brought the card into sharp focus and saw the ragged fibrous texture of the paper's surface. Sliding the card, he scanned for the mysterious spot until it dramatically swept into view. It was apparently a spot of ink, but its shape, like a Rorschach blotch, registered suddenly with Carl.

It was a profile of Amanda, but with a long arrow flying out of her mouth. A jarring image. He lifted his eyes to look out the window and search for something, anything, to take his attention away from the image. A hibiscus bush in the foreground twisted in the breeze. The sturdy plant, which survived despite Carl's benign neglect, was festooned with pale pink blossoms.

Carl's gaze intensified as he considered one of the flowers. *It was thriving, as only it knew how,* he thought.

At this realization, he closed his eyes and then burst into laughter. The ink blotch wasn't Amanda; it was he.

The phone rang. He hoped it was her. "Hello," he answered.

"Carl, I want to apologize for being so harsh."

"I am so glad you called. Don't worry; I decided I just need to prepare myself better before I talk about something like that," he said.

"I don't want you to have to prepare yourself to talk to me," she said. "I want you to feel safe to talk about anything."

Those words were like a balm applied to his bruised ego, but his ego was tender only because it had bloated, inflated by insecurity. And now he knew that he didn't want to honor the insecurity: It was time to thrive, as only he knew how, and not relative to Amanda or anyone else. Only then, he finally realized, could he unconditionally love her and himself without any leaps of faith.

He decided that this revelation was cause to celebrate. "Let's go back to the coffee shop and order one of those eclairs," he said enthusiastically.

"Great!" said Amanda.

Then Carl added, "But give me a few extra minutes. I'm going to the car wash."

INTERVIEW WITH AN ANGEL

THERE WAS A CRISP KNOCK AT THE DOOR. WALTER PLACED HIS unfinished croissant on its plate, stood, and brushed the crumbs off of his white tunic. Straightening the tunic and tightening its sash, he briskly paced to the door. Swinging it open, the visitor announced, "Hello, I'm Garth—"

But he was quickly interrupted by Walter, who continued, "—Reynolds from the Daily Hyperion. I've been expecting you. Please come in!"

Garth walked through the arched entrance and followed Walter, who threaded through the pillars to his breakfast table as he spoke. "Would you care for a croissant? Espresso?" Looking at the seven-foot tall metallic sentinel that floated nearby, he continued, "Amos is very handy in the kitchen."

"That's quite alright," replied Garth. "If it's ok with you, I'd like to start with our interview." He turned on his recorder.

"Of course." Turning to Amos, Walter commanded, "Tidy up!" at which Amos whirred to life and sprouted spindly articulated arms with crablike grips. The arms whizzed and the grips clicked as the table's contents were dispatched. Garth leaned back as the appendages raced by, eliciting a great laugh from Walter. "Amos couldn't possibly hurt you!" Walter smiled as the robot floated into the kitchen. "Unless all of your credits were spent, of course. Now, shall we start the interview? I must confess to being a bit nervous." His sky blue eyes gazed down to the spotless table, a self-conscious chill stifling his enthusiasm.

Garth smiled. He knew that look, the look of someone's first interview, of that hope for notoriety rather than humiliation. "Let's just start with a summary of the role of an angel."

Walter looked up. "I supposed that all of your readers already know that." Lacking a reply from Garth, Walter continued, "Well, to summarize, angels keep the peace and maximize the happiness of society. That is our charter, so to speak." With a flourish of his hands, he added, "It's how angels make the world better each and every day!"

"That's very nice," said Garth. "That's a beautiful robe you are wearing. Tell me about your uniform."

"Ever since the angel class was established many years ago, each angel has worn a tunic, like mine. They all look like this, white with the sash around the waist. I suppose you'd say it's our uniform. Because an angel is on duty all of the time, we wear it all day." He smiled. "I have seven of them, one for each day of the week, even though they are all the same." His eyes searched the room as if to find any more thoughts. "That's about it. Oh, naturally, we carry the Plex as we make our rounds."

"What's the Plex?"

A leather-bound case, the size of a hardcover book, hung at the angel's side by a shoulder strap. He lifted the unit to show its small shiny screen. "The Plex here awards credits and demerits, as the angel sees fit. If I see somebody do a good deed, say, picking up a piece of litter, then I would ask them to place their thumb on the screen. That permits me to award them for the deed, say two credits for picking up a small piece of litter. It's a nice way to say, 'Well done!'"

"What about the person who tossed the litter?"

"I thought you'd ask that! Well, it kind of works in the opposite direction. They place their thumb and two credits are removed."

"What if they don't want to place their thumb? They may just run away." Looking at the diminutive angel, he said, "And, Walter, you may not be able to outrun them."

Walter swiveled his chair and gestured to Amos. "I get a little help from my friend. Each angel is paired with a machine like Amos."

"I see… your friend is certainly impressive. May I take a picture of the two of you?" Walter gladly complied and posed beside the floating giant. When the picture was taken, Garth continued, "How did you become an angel?"

Walter thought and said, "Every angel has had their own journey. It's like climbing a tree: the starting and ending places are clear, but the connecting paths are just found as you go. As for mine, it was very simple, I suppose. I always liked to keep track of my credits, checking every few days… like owning stock. And I strived to end the month with more credits than I started with." He chuckled. "There were a few months when, you know, I had slipped bit and was afraid I'd break my winning streak. Once, I had to gain 85 credits in two days. Well, I tell you I was busy. There's always an angel at Midland Park, so I picked all of the litter and got 35 credits. I knew where angels guarded and I worked the system, you might say, although please don't write that. I don't like how it sounds."

"Go on," said Garth.

"Goodness, I walked old ladies across the street, volunteered at the soup kitchen, and I don't know what all. Well, long story short, I got 90 credits in those two days!" He beamed triumphantly. "I just naturally enjoy earning credits. Eventually, I averaged over 500 credits per year. Born with 1000, I hit the required 10,000 for Angelhood by my 30th birthday. One of the youngest!"

Walter continued, "I love this job! For example, yesterday was great! I awarded 435 credits and only 126 demerits." He paused, gazing out the window. "One of those demerits was kinda tough. The guy was already down to seven credits and he ran a red light." He paused, turning to Garth. "That's 100 demerits."

"Oh," said Garth, fearing the next sentence.

"He's gone now. Amos just took care of it right then and there. No pain. They train you for this, so I was ready, you know, for the bargaining. The wife, she has over 1200 credits and she was like, "Take mine. The kids need their father… that sort of thing." He stared earnestly at Garth: "What makes a man get down to seven credits, anyway?"

"Born with 1000 and lose 993," was all Garth could muster.

"Well, all in a day's work! Have I said that I love this job?"

Shaken, Garth shifted gears. "So, what do you do to unwind?"

"Unwind? Oh, if I have to relax?"

"Yeah, like yesterday. You eliminated a human being."

Suddenly stern, Walter said, "Point of information: He eliminated himself." Smiling again, he continued, "But, to your question, I fancy standup!"

"You don't mean comedy?"

"I do! Don't you like comedy? Everyone likes to laugh!"

Garth wondered how many long years would pass before anyone in the family of that man would laugh. "Sure," Garth hesitated. "Tell me a joke."

Walter's eyes brightened; he obviously relished the request. Clearly, this would justify hosting a nosy reporter in his dining room. "Didja hear the one about the newborn baby who asked how many credits he had left?"

Silence. Garth leaned forward, anticipating a punch line. "I give up, what did the baby say?"

Walter burst into laughter. "Don't ya get it? It's a double joke! Newborn babies can't talk and they always have 1000 credits!"

The reporter managed a polite smile, but Walter was clearly disappointed.

"What else do you have?" asked Garth.

"Well, here's another one!" He cheered up again, pushed away from the table and stood up. "It's stand up," he affirmed.

"Yes," said Garth.

"Two angels walk into a bar—that's not the joke," he explained, "Angels can't drink—but, anyway, they walk into this bar and ask, 'When is happy hour?'

"'That depends,' says the bartender. 'How many credits you gonna give me?'"

There was a long pause. Walter absorbed the reporter's sour reaction, but he soldiered on, saying, "Tough crowd."

"Don't quit your day job." Garth smiled.

The comment landed like a punch to the stomach. Still standing, Walter took several deep breaths. "Angels maximize happiness," he slowly repeated, fixing his stare at Garth. "If someone doesn't want to be happy, that works against us."

Garth could feel a toxic mixture of fear and anger well up. He shifted in his seat. Maintaining a cool façade, he said, "Some say that you cannot shape a person's morals with barbed wire, that a person will do what they are compelled to do. Tell someone a joke is funny and credit them for laughing, but don't for a moment believe they were amused. They say a society can act moral even if it's not."

"Who says this? Where do they live?" demanded Walter.

Garth couldn't form a reply before Walter exploded, "I think they live in *your* house. I think it's *you!*"

Garth paled, as Walter hollered, pointing a stern finger: "I will not tolerate this. Behave!"

"Or what?" blurted Garth. An icy wave of fear washed over him. What was he saying? What an idiot!

"Or what?" Walter repeated, now possessed by quiet confidence. "Please present your right thumb."

At the top of the bullet-like robot, three red lights came to life and a whirring sound started deep in its interior.

Garth swallowed. His hand shook as he extended it.

"Kindly press it to the screen," requested Walter. Garth complied. Walter glanced down at the machine, saying, "Tsk, don't worry... five demerits won't matter to you. You have 327 credits." The machine quickly chimed five times. "Well, 322 now. Thank you." Amos fell silent, lights quenched.

Garth pulled back his hand.

Walter was reflexively composed. He was a being in whose veins flowed orthodoxy. "Now that the unpleasantness is passed, would you like to hear more stand up?"

Garth calculated. "Why, yes, I would like to hear more."

With a broad smile, Walter asked, "How many angels does it take to screw in a light bulb?"

Garth roared with manufactured laughter.

Walter shrieked, "Get out! Get out before I clear your account!"

Garth pushed away from the table, grabbed his recorder, and raced to the door. He flung it open and scrambled down the wide lawn to his craft. He quickly boarded and it sprang to life. It shot vertically and then whisked away.

Back inside the house, a breeze blew through the door past Walter, who collapsed into his chair. Lips pouting, he slipped off the Plex and stared at the machine on the table before him. He fumed, fingers gripping it. "He's wrong, it's wrong!" His eyes squeezed shut and tears tracked down his face. His cloaked body trembled with rage. He began to pound the table with the machine, nails digging deeply into the leather. "It can't be this way!" He pounded harder, repeating, "Right is right!" again and again, building to a crescendo. He took a deep breath, screamed, and flung the machine at Amos, shattering the Plex.

Amos whizzed to life, red lights blazing.

QUANTUM EMBRACE

BRIGHT SUN WAS SHINING THROUGH THE AUBURN LEAVES ON the third day of Carl and Amanda's road trip through northern New England. Out to see the fall colors, it had been a pleasant getaway; they smiled easily and enjoyed driving through the small towns. Carl, in particular, had wound down until his normally tight main spring was nearly slack. He was on the electrical engineering academic faculty, but a steady diet of analysis could result in a kind of intellectual scurvy. A balanced diet called for variety of interests, which, for Carl, included the familiar, such as hiking, and, in those rare occasions when time and motivation aligned, creating short animated cartoons. But a road trip escape like this was the remedy when all else failed.

After hours driving through endless coniferous forests, Carl behind the wheel, he suddenly slipped into his playful radio promotional voice and excitedly said, "'Ufee and the Cosmonauts', starring Zenobia as the boatlock!"

"What's a boatlock?" Amanda frowned.

"I don't know," replied Carl, "Go see the cartoon! I just announce them."

"You are going to make a new cartoon?" she enthused.

"No comment," came the crisp reply, as Carl reflected on the effort to make a cartoon. But he continued the whimsical monologue.

71

"What if we could send a giant mirror into space? Imagine a mirror so huge, so flat, and so distant that it would take light maybe an hour to make the round trip. Then, from telescopes on Earth we could see what had happened an hour ago. It would be like instant replay for the entire planet. We could look at traffic accidents as they happened, examine a crime scene as the crime occurred..."

"As long as it happened outside on a clear sunny day," interjected Amanda.

"... as long as it happened outside on a clear and sunny day," he continued, "And if the mirror was a light year away, you could see things that happened two years ago."

"You're ignoring quantum effects."

"Well, I'll let you work out that detail," said Carl. Amanda laughed as he continued, "But we could try from one of the new Moon bases! The university has some slots open!"

"Oh! Yes!", cheered Amanda.

"Just think", he said, "Everyone's biography would be played back for anyone to see. The light from all of our lives now just flies out into space forever, lost forever. But the space mirror would change all of that. Imagine if there was a mirror 100 light years away. We could watch Beethoven argue with Goethe in Vienna, or Jefferson walking around Monticello."

"Who would have launched that mirror? Woops, sorry. I guess that's another detail for me."

"Yeah!"

"It's a wonderful idea, Carl. But don't you think there are scenes from your biography you'd rather not see again, or rather not have anyone else see?"

Carl thought for a moment. "I suppose so. For starters, I think I'd want to skip the teenybopper years, some of them anyway. And I wouldn't want anyone else to see those, either."

"Me, too," she said. "We were so self-conscious as teenagers. It's almost as though just thinking about those years makes us self-conscious all over again. Seems unfair."

"So, do you still like the idea?" he asked.

"Oh, definitely! So what if there are scenes from our past we don't want to relive? They are part of who we are."

Carl replied, "Yeah, but you don't see a picture in my house of my dad when he was drunk. That's part of my past, but I am quite content for it to be shelved. Not forgotten, but not in my face, either."

Amanda put her arm around him. "So... what to show and what to hide?"

"Maybe it's just as well that the light of our lives eventually becomes fuzzy and lost in a haze," he said.

- A *Bit* More than a Year Later -

Carl bounced gracefully across the studio dug into regolith at the lunar south pole. He floated into his seat at the drawing table, which was wired to his animation workstation, and resumed his watercolor painting. It was a critical scene in his cartoon, "Ufee and the Cosmonauts," and Carl wanted to make sure the background illustration of the sparkling Milky Way was icy and foreboding, rather than spectacular or awe inspiring. Ufee was in the midst of her daring escape from the cosmonauts' secret asteroid lair. From over Carl's head, reflected sunlight shined down a lightwell and flooded the table. Light at the lunar south pole was always indirect because the sun scarcely rose above the craggy horizon. Peering up the lightwell, Carl studied his subject as the stunning Milky Way shone in stark contrast to the undiluted inky black. He applied the finishing touches to the canvas.

"Have you figured out what a boatlock is yet?" Amanda called from her workbench across the room.

Carl was a bit tense as he replied, "No, and I have to figure it out fast. I've put it off about as long as I can. I decided that Ufee is going to use one to escape. How is the space mirror?"

"I am expecting first light soon. The mirror is right overhead, about 30 light-minutes away, so we'll see scenes from our happy Lunar home from about an hour ago."

"Outstanding!" said Carl, smiling broadly, before re-immersing himself in his animated dilemma.

Amanda and Carl worked in their separate worlds, but these were worlds that closely and eternally orbited each other.

Carl resolved his dilemma. He decided Ufee would use a space "boat" to leave the asteroid. *That works,* he thought to himself. She would have to befriend a cantankerous android named Zenobia, whose current job was to keep the boat secured. Zenobia was lonely and welcomed attention, and Carl figured that Ufee could…

"Carl! It's coming! First light!" exclaimed Amanda. Carl pushed away from the table and bounded to Amanda's workbench.

A powerful and revolutionary telescope was trained on the distant mirror. An extremely high-resolution monitor displayed the first light: A view of the south pole sufficiently magnified to see the house and surrounding structures. The image was softened by the quantum losses from the light's long round trip but details were clearly visible.

"I'm going to zoom in!" said Amanda. Turning a dial, the image of the house rapidly grew to fill the screen.

"There's the lightwell!" said Carl, pointing. "Let's look down there!" Amanda carefully used the controls to pan to the lightwell, which appeared as a circular disk of artificial light, then zoomed to peer into it. Carl's empty canvas for the Milky Way background was plainly visible. His hands were gesturing, making sweeping motions across the canvas. "That's when I was explaining to you how I wanted the background to look," he said.

Amanda paused before responding, eyes now fixed on the finished canvas, biting her lip. She whispered in a voice so gentle and demure that Carl could scarcely hear her over the background hum of equipment, "And that was just before you said that you loved me."

Carl felt as though his entire life, if not the entire universe, had existed for this moment. He squeezed her hand and gazed at her radiant face. She continued, still staring at the canvas, but now allowing a coy smile, "I guess you didn't love me when the first light left." Amanda drew courage from the deepest well within her and turned toward Carl with a broad smile, saying, "Even though I feel like I have loved you forever."

Then the replay from space showed Amanda lean over the canvas toward Carl, who leaned forward to meet her. Over the empty canvas they kissed in a fuzzy embrace. And then, in the crystal clarity of the present, Carl gently pulled Amanda to him and they held each other close for a thousand years.

FLIGHT OF FANCY

ELOISE SAT IN THE CORNER, HER TOYS GROUPED AROUND HER. It was warm; she was bored and squirming. Her eyes fastened on the yo-yo. She lurched over and yanked on the unraveled string. The red toy jolted into the air, bounced off the wall, and landed on her lap. Eloise laughed. Wrapping a length of string around her fat finger, she began to whirl the toy overhead, careening it off the walls, marking them with random red scars. The wild chaos of the ricocheting projectile increased in tempo until the yo-yo collided squarely with her runny nose. She defiantly unwound the string from her finger and punished the toy by throwing it at a fire truck but hit a horse, instead.

Eloise dug into her toy box under a mountain of treasures and grasped the edge of a silver flying saucer. She heaved the long entombed saucer out of its premature grave. The bottom of the disc had orange dots arranged in a circle. Eloise made a buzzing sound as she lowered it to eye level. She held it there to study, squinting her eyes to make out the shadowy details behind a band of narrow windows. Pink glossy anthropoids peered cautiously through the window openings. A wall-mounted television monitor had unpeeled and was leaning against a soldier. In the murky darkness, a ladder descended into an agonizing unknown. Eloise rested the saucer on her lap. She closed her eyes and then she smiled. After several quiet moments, Eloise was asleep.

Down the ladder, in the shadowy depths of the lower chamber, a shape tentatively stirred. The shape's silhouette vaguely contrasted against the pitch-black background as it cautiously rose from a chair and stood. The creature waited. It strained to listen and when it heard Eloise's deep, rhythmic breathing, its flexible limbs stretched toward the ladder. In the filtered light, pink digits at the end of one tentacled hand slowly wrapped around a rung. It paused again to confirm that it was safe to proceed, safe to climb. In the other hand, a polished silver sphere was tightly gripped.

Like a stalking cat that moves only when prey is unaware, the creature took careful steps in synch with Eloise's breaths until its pink, glossy head emerged through the opening. Light! Outside the windows was light for the first time in years! Black eyespots flitted at the chaotic scene on the main deck.

With calibrated, incremental motion, the creature lifted itself onto the main deck, pausing, listening, and carefully advancing. It gazed at the silver sphere wrapped by its shiny digits. Across the chamber was an oval control panel and, in its center, a concave receptacle for the sphere.

The creature moved carefully next to the leaning soldier. "Zvvv… Trrr," whispered the lead creature to the soldier. The soldier animated, stood erect, looked at the creature, and nodded deferentially. The creature showed the soldier the sphere, gestured toward the concave slot, and whispered again. The soldier acknowledged and proceeded to awaken the others as the lead creature slowly advanced toward the control panel.

With the creature's flexible arm extended to place the sphere, the awakened crew stared, eyespots all riveted on the sphere. An "achooo!" exploded outside and the saucer shook. The crew froze; Eloise yawned.

Bleary eyes peered through the windows and widened in disbelief at the rearranged deck scene. The creature, arm extended, kept still but its eyespots reflexively shifted to lock onto Eloise's gaze as she stared at it. She screamed and threw the saucer into the toy box. The creature fought the inertia to keep its balance and strained to place the sphere into the control panel but Eloise scrambled to rebury the saucer. The crew heard the avalanche rumbling above and the saucer pitched as Eloise piled a mountain of toys over the craft.

In the distance, the heavy toy chest lid fell like a mighty thunderclap. The world grew still, silent and pitch black again.

The crew steadied themselves in the angled saucer. As though awakened momentarily from a coma, the crew was reminded of their plight. And they slowly returned into brittle shapes, as hope receded once again.

ISAAC'S CHANGE
OF REFERENCE

ISAAC LIVED FOR HIS VISITS TO THE CITY LIBRARY AND ONCE
again he breezed through the entrance to its expansive main floor.
Beyond the Circulation Department, past phalanxes of shelving,
around tables that displayed the latest acquisitions or arcane
thematic collections, was his favorite chair by the Reference Desk.
He threaded to his destination, where he plopped down with a sigh.
For Isaac didn't come to the library for books or periodicals. This
sour curmudgeon came to witness idiocy and the Reference Desk
was Ground Zero. Not that he had ever used its services – far from it.
Rather, he was a regular irritant to the dedicated, and it must be said,
efficient librarian who handled the phoned-in reference questions. It
fed Isaac's pseudointellectual ego to hear the often-peculiar answers.
The librarian knew his snickers and disparaging comments; she knew
to soldier on when Isaac was in his chair.

To Isaac, hearing one side of these conversations was entertaining
enough to justify the visit. For example:

"A Humboldt squid."

"Fidelity Select Chemical was up 0.3%."

"Joe DiMaggio."

"I am sorry, sir, but you are only permitted three questions per day... thank you!"

Chuckling to himself, Isaac wondered, *How was that part of a coherent conversation? Who are these lunatics?* It seemed there was an unlimited supply of halfwits. After all, who phones a Reference Desk to check the price of their stock? He cackled, shaking his head in disbelief while he waited expectantly for the next performance. He wasn't disappointed.

"Fred and Wilma"

"Gravitational lensing"

"Yes, water is gluten-free."

Isaac laughed out loud, which once again drew scorn from the Reference Desk librarian. So what? He had to listen to her; she could hear him, too! These one-sided conversations reminded him of attempts to converse with unhinged street people. Their minds often were a crazy quilt of random ideas stitched together. Thermodynamics might lead to presidential politics and then to trout fishing. To a misanthropic soul like Isaac, that was a hoot.

The callers never disappointed and he lost count until it was time for an especially memorable inquiry.

"Hello, this is the Reference Desk. May I help you?" This was followed by a longer than usual pause before the first answer:

"Isaac Blochman".

Wait! That was his name! He sat bolt upright and fixed his gaze at the librarian. She listened intently to the caller, who must have been explaining a complex idea. Seconds ticked like hours before the librarian answered the second question:

"No, a cyanide blow dart is more lethal."

Isaac abruptly stood and marched to the desk to listen carefully. He leaned in front of the librarian as she paid dutiful attention to the caller. Then came the third answer:

"Correct: The United States has no extradition treaty with Cameroon." This was followed by a particularly cheerful, "Why, that sounds *lovely*! You have a nice day, too... Goodbye!"

The librarian hung up the phone and acted surprised to notice Isaac leaning over the desk. His drumming fingertips stomped in tiny puddles of sweat. With a warm smile, she pleasantly asked, "May I help you?"

"Who was that caller!?" he spat.

"Pardon me?" she replied, taken aback. "We don't ask the caller's name."

Fists clenched, he stared with barely contained rage and said, "Listen to me." She responded with a sweet grin. That triggered his explosive reply, "I am Isaac Blochman!"

Heads turned across the whole floor.

The librarian leaned back in her chair and clasped her hands over her heart. "Oh dear!" came the dramatic response. "Mr. Blochman! I think it would be in your best interest to leave… quite promptly, in fact!"

Isaac was gone in a flash, never to return, much to the librarian's delight.

THE JOURNEY OF ARLENE THE SQUID

RLENE WAS A YOUNG SQUID THAT LIVED IN THE IMMEDIATE proximity of a seething volcanic vent under three miles of mid-Atlantic ocean. To say that life was simple for her would be an overt understatement.

Only two other kinds of creatures shared her inky environs, the passive sea worms and the tenuous clouds of brine they strained from the sluggish water. Arlene, who also subsisted on inhaled brine, was not only the most locomotive resident but, by her appraisal, the most intelligent. Her presence in the locale was a fluke of the first magnitude. As a pea-sized translucent egg she was split off from a blade of kelp by the deep residual currents of hurricane Arlene, her namesake. She managed to survive a slow, tortuous decent down a column of water warmed by volcanic exhaust. Now Arlene would jet about her pitch-dark world with childhood glee in the fragile zone between the searing vent and the frigid expanse. She would dart close to the belching hearth, then deftly jet away until she glided close to the numbing outer boundary. She could play this game forever! She decided it was her fate to cut zigzagging orbits around this submarine volcanic vent.

After countless circuits around the vent, Arlene's imperturbable bliss was jarred as she accidentally grazed a plume of superheated water. She reeled back, more from shock than the stinging pain. She continued on her repetitive route and discounted the incident as an anomaly. After several more laps, her peace of mind had been almost completely restored when she suddenly plowed into deep iciness. She rocketed back but then blundered past the boiling cauldron. She tried to steady herself in the belt of comfortable warmth but, while her face was pitched in coldness, her tentacles were dancing to relieve the heat. Arlene was mortified. And then she reached a sobering realization: she was growing to maturity.

And so, her soul laden with sadness, Arlene issued half-hearted downward squirts and slowly ascended from her private, blissful domain. Her depression deepened as she climbed, because this new world was so oppressively drab. There was no fuming core and the iciness spread farther away. Arlene floated through the dark in perfect stillness. Her long flexible body was being carried by the faint dissipated surges of the familiar vent and her mind was turned completely inward, locked in droning confusion and then, ultimately, forlorn resignation.

Suddenly, she was shaken from her withdrawal in a stunning panic. Her mind became wildly acrobatic as it tried to comprehend a spectacular new experience. There was absolutely nothing that this incredible event could remind her of. Her panic swelled simultaneously with giddy excitement.

Arlene could see. Through a frustrating murkiness, she gazed at herself for the first time and could make out light and dark markings along her elegantly tapered body. She wanted to see more. She heaved and ejected herself higher. She saw the first subtle hints of pink and tan that colored her. She pushed again and saw the suction cups that lined her tentacles. She pushed harder again and again, and, from her brush with the inferno, she could see the scar; she could see the fine texture in her skin. Arlene surged upward in repeated frenzied blasts, her tentacles whipping the water. She aimed for the distant apex of the widening cone of light that showered around her. She rocketed faster as the water thinned and then the sea itself took on color. It was as though the entire world was filled with color! Schools of shimmering fish shifted and turned in perfect choreography. The agitated silvery underside of the surface scattered dazzling patterns across kelp forests. Striped giants lumbered through the cyan expanse as she surged, nearing exhaustion. As her world gradually turned warm and brilliant, Arlene's pushes slowed and then ceased.

Once again she drifted perfectly still; this time her mind was alive with fascination of the terrifically kinetic world of which she was now a part.

MERRY MINT

I WAS REMINDED OF THE RAGGED HOLE IN MY PANTS POCKET when the coins from my Hershey bar purchase dribbled down my leg and onto the platform of the merry-go-round. As the great wheel spun, my hands slipped on the greasy brass pole that anchored my bounding zebra. This animal was sized for a child instead of a misplaced paunchy office worker on an idiotic escapade. For one extended lunch break, I was AWOL from my ham-handed manager at a job that squeezed me lifeless as a bloom wedged between the pages of a book, a book at the bottom of a stack, a stack that grew each day as he added to the pile. I was frantic to run away, but I could only hold tight as I spun in circles.

I wiped sweaty palms in frantic zigzags across my crisp white shirt. The clattering coins maintained an unsteady balance as they rolled and bounced outward from the hub of the spinning contraption. The racket triggered the avarice of every child in sight. "I saw them first!" "Mine!" They rained down from bobbing horses and giraffes and unicorns in a frenzied scramble for my money. Elbows jabbed, hooves scraped, and fists punched as the children fought each other as much as the centrifugal force that shoved them away from the center.

I would have ordered them to stop, if I thought anyone would heed my words. Why expect any more authority here than where I earn a salary?

The operator of our rotating world, like my manager, was a grizzled and bulky chap. I could catch a glance of him with each revolution, though he only stared straight ahead from an overburdened chair parked next to the spinning platform. He had seen it all, and every day, with every revolution, he saw it again. But this moment interrupted the flow. The operator's hand rested on the end of the control stick and, with a casual pull of the brake lever, the merry-go-round decelerated. The children were thrown off-balance and the coins abruptly changed course. Deftly avoiding the jungle of protruding hooves and horns, the children landed on the platform. As the great wheel jerked to a halt, I saw my coins roll in a single file over the edge of the platform. And then I heard them strike the operator's black dusty boot. *One—two—three—four.*

The operator peered down at the coins and then lifted his head to consider the misfit who lost them. I dismounted my zebra. He bent over, picked up the coins, and then dropped them into his pants pocket. The children turned their heads to stare at me. The operator tightened his grip on the control stick as I stepped toward him. I paused to summon courage; alas, none replied, so I turned back and remounted my little steed. Seeing this, the children clambered up to their places on their animals. Then we waited, silent, obedient, and attentive. The operator took a moment to wallow in his miniature victory and then smirked as he eased back on the accelerator.

And as the world once again began to spin, we could hear his laugh orbit us like the full moon hanging in the sky behind him.

RET*MOG:
AN ABSURD NARRATIVE

MY RIGHT FOOT ACHED. THE SOLID METAL JAWS OF THE horrible machine held it firmly. My other foot, still throbbing from the pressure exerted on it by the second set of jaws, was beginning to emerge from numbness when, just like before, the machine simultaneously released my right foot, and gripped my left foot again. The sudden rush of blood to the freed foot caused my toes to pound. The left foot quickly numbed and I waited for the horrible cycle to proceed.

There was never enough time after the jaws released one foot for it to fully regain sensation. This sorry fact made escape impossible for, unless I could manage to remain delicately balanced on the top of the menacing vices, l would risk falling uncontrollably into their path. The possibility of being summarily squeezed beyond repair and all recognition was untenable. So, I remained a prisoner. Such was the penalty of giving in to my impulsive nature when I decided to find a shortcut from my house to the Ret*Mog Store. Why I was prompted on this particular night, this typically sensuous summer evening, to avoid crossing the rope bridge and instead make my way into the valley would be a matter of debate for me for some time to come, I suppose. Of course, now I was going to be late and Grace would most likely be upset with me. She usually waited for me after she got off work at the store, but I'd never tested her to see just how long she would wait.

The jaws began to relax. After several cycles, neither foot ever slipped entirely into numbness and I was slowly building up the confidence to try leaping on top of the jaws to begin my escape. Perhaps that jump wasn't going to be necessary if the jaws stopped all together, hopefully with neither foot locked in eternal embrace. The jaws grinded to a halt and I lifted my feet out of their path, thus sparing me from interminable duress. I shuffled toward the edge of the flat metal roof on top of which this drama had transpired. My feet responded to my commands sluggishly. I was certain that all but the nerves buried deep in the interiors of my feet had been successively frayed and sheared.

As I neared the ledge, colors from the lights below presented themselves, softened by the characteristic heaviness of the evening air. The colors were familiar to me. They were the yellow, orange, and pink that emblazoned the great Ret*Mog sign mounted above the store's entrance. As I neared the edge, it all began to make sense that I was on top of the store and that, by climbing down the letters in the sign, I could lower myself to the pavement safely. I reached the edge and peered down, moved by the perilous drop that awaited me should I misstep or otherwise blunder. I was situated about five feet above the "M." Now that I was leaning over the edge, the convective heat from the lights in the sign swam around my head and my nostrils. There was also the rude oily stench of the vehicles idling on the pavement, their exhaust being fanned upward by the sign and slamming into the most inaccessible confines of my sinuses.

I rolled my feet over the edge and onto the top of the letter. Shifting my weight from one foot to the other, I tested the solidity of my feet and the sign. All were at least adequate. I sat on the uncomfortably warm letter, my feet now slung down onto the diagonal from the vertical member of the letter toward its middle. Looking down the steep ramp, I could see the joint of the diagonals twenty feet away. Somebody appeared to have lobbed onto the diagonal what was at one time probably a cool rich milk beverage but which was now a thin viscous brown-gray stain. I resolved to try and avoid the stain at all costs. I slowly lowered myself onto the diagonal, pressing my feet against its surface to hold me in place.

Suddenly, I felt two terribly sharp spikes of pain in the ankles of both feet. I reeled in pain, involuntarily lifting my feet from the diagonal that caused me to slide uncontrollably toward the stain. As I gained speed, I imparted well-directed blows onto the letter with my hands in an attempt to steer myself away from the stain. My efforts met with only partial success. While half of my posterior missed the stain, the other half slid into it and immediately slowed, causing the clean half to pivot around squarely into the stain despite my best attempts. The stain, unfortunately, was not viscous enough to bring me to a halt.

Now I was headed on a due course off the front of the letter. My arms and legs flailing, I screamed madly as I soared away from the "M" and began rocketing toward the unforgiving pavement below. Oceans of yellow, orange, and pink lights danced before my eyes. Below, I could see herds of cars and customers squealing to avoid the predicted point of impact. A rotund woman abandoned her full shopping cart, which proceeded to roll under me.

My back slammed into a small mountain of root beer and ice cream. The sudden impact yielded a spherical blast wave of saccharine mist that was tinted orange by the brilliant sign. My body was bent but not broken as the compression cushioned the fall.

I turned to see Grace emerge from the lingering mist, transfixed at the horror of her friend conformed to the crushed shopping cart. I appeared relaxed on a post-modern chaise lounge, but as viewed via a funhouse mirror.

"Am I late?" I heard myself ask.

But before she could answer, I was seduced by sleep or perhaps I had succumbed to concussion.

Maybe I had died.

SIMON'S ESCAPE

IMON WAS EXILED TO THE LEFT SIDE OF HIS BRAIN. HE FELT cursed to live the life of an analyst, never to take a skinny-dipping plunge into the effervescent pool of self-expression. Al Capone's prison cell on Alcatraz was said to have had a view of the San Francisco marina. On balmy summer nights, he could hear the parties from the glittering city through the bars. Locked in the left side of his brain, Simon could only imagine what thrills might await him if he could saw through the bars and escape.

The warden of Simon's prison was a humorless hulk named Ned ("Nyet," to Simon). Ned patrolled the grounds with slavish vigilance. He existed for two reasons: to make sure Simon fulfilled all of his responsibilities, and to make sure he remained prepared for all contingencies. Ned kept visitors to a precious few, always standing guard, alternately tapping his nightstick and checking his watch until it was time to quickly escort the visitor out the gates.

In one of Simon's more popular fantasies, Ned is pacing in front of his cell. He suddenly keels over dead, the ring of keys conveniently in reach. Simon unlocks the cage door and swings it open, clunking it against Ned's heavy crewcut-crowned skull. Here, the fantasies diverged.

Usually, Simon boards a dinghy and departs his Alcatraz to seek pent up adventure and gratification in the San Francisco of his right brain. But sometimes he stands on the stony Alcatraz shore. He stares at the dinghy, wondering if it has leaks. Are there really sharks in the water? How cold is it? He searches for life preservers. He goes back for Ned's wallet. He plans. He optimizes. He gets tired and hungry. He steps into his cell for a bite to eat and to think about next steps. When he falls asleep, he is awakened by the icy clang of the cage door shut by a revitalized Ned.

Or he climbs into the dinghy and paddles across, through fog banks and by great gray shapes that sail past and churn the water so he is nearly tipped out. The dinghy crunches into the sandy shore and Simon springs out and climbs up to the roadside. He is NOT struck by a car. He is NOT paralyzed with fear. Ned is NOT there waiting. Rather, he bounds across the street, his soggy feet making each step feel electric. He sprints up the steep incline, stops to catch his breath, then starts again, and flies toward whatever is over the top of the hill and forever away from the island that disappears into the fog like a childhood nightmare.

He settles into life. He finds a niche, a warm and healthy place to finally learn how to be Simon. Trepidation is dwarfed by exhilaration and with every breath of free air, his world expands and he sheds the old routines like a drab and tired coat. He becomes as Simon as he can be, being Simon out loud, Simon in vivid color and harmony. And for a few minutes one summer afternoon, he pauses on his transit to write this story.

A CRIMSON CIRCLE

CASPER SQUINTED THROUGH THE CRIMSON CIRCLE OF GLASS. HE paused, scratched his white-stubbled chin, and then picked up a maroon glass triangle. He passed the two pieces through his gaze back and forth several times before finally placing the maroon piece on his workbench, upon a heap of other red-hued glass fragments. Looking at the crimson circle, he said, "My apple."

In his windswept seaside bungalow, Casper worked in the basement, piecing together a stained glass masterwork. A window opening had been prepared in the attic, which had been converted into a small study. The wall with the strongest sunlight was also the wall with the view over the verdant hills to the ocean. That view would soon be replaced by an iridescent image of the Garden of Eden, with Adam and Eve vanquishing the serpent underfoot. Occasionally, Casper would climb the roughhewn stairs to the study, two flights from the basement. He would go to the opening, which was shuttered with a sheet of plywood, and swing it open. The fresh wind would blow through his white hair and would loosen the dust in the room. As he gazed, his eyes would tear, sometimes from the bracing breeze, but sometimes from the bittersweetness of replacing the sweeping view with his image of Eden. It was a decision he had wrestled with, and decided would never be settled: Was his ideal in any way a fitting replacement for the scene of such common grandeur?

Over the weeks as he cut, soldered, and pieced together his mosaic, the scene breathed to life. Adam and Eve, their backs to the tree, ground the serpent lifeless. Behind them, the crimson apple hung from the tree. "It's too much," he would say to himself. He would stop, fold his arms, and his face would wrench in disappointment. After some thoughtful moments, the strength of his conviction would rise to the strength of the scene spread out on the workbench, and he would resume his work. Soon it would be framed and ready to be carried upstairs. He worried about it shattering before the sunlight passed through. A misstep from the basement to the attic and it could be lost. But what would really be lost, he thought? And what would be kept? It was certainly a risk worth taking.

Finally, with a gingerly placed cyan polygon, he soldered the last fragment to the sky and the spectacle was complete. The solder cooled. Casper wedged his creation into the grooves of a solid oak frame and tapped the frame lightly with a hammer to ensure the fit was snug and secure. It was now time for the momentous trip to the attic study. Casper carefully hefted the loaded frame, keeping it vertical so as to not strain the intricate solder web. He walked to the base of the stairs, checked his footing, and began the climb.

Each step out of the basement was measured and soon he emerged into the hallway on the ground floor. Sunlight filtered in from the bedroom windows and Casper tried to hold up the frame to catch the light, but it was ponderous and caused his arms to shake. He pulled it closer to him and continued to the attic stairs, swinging the door open with his foot. These stairs were narrow and steep and though his arms were starting to tremble from bearing the weight, he didn't want to stop his progress. He climbed, stretching to each new step with shaking legs. He could feel his shoulders tightening and his palms sweating but he could also now see the prepared opening in the wall, sunlight streaming, and he steeled his resolve and pressed on to the top. Reaching the summit, he gently rested the frame on the floor beneath the opening. He collapsed like a slack-stringed marionette and rested.

After a pause to collect his strength, he stood, gripped the frame once more and, with newfound strength, lifted it into place. The fit was impeccable. While he held it firmly with one hand, he slipped the frame onto a set of hinges he had mounted to the wall. Hinges, he had decided, would grant him both a view of his ideal and of the common grandeur outside. He mounted a latch and tested it. The window shut tightly. The sun radiated the scene and flooded the attic with saturated chromatic splashes. A crimson beam from the apple painted Casper's sweaty forehead. He smiled and retired to the comfortable chair he positioned to gaze at, or through, the window.

In the months and years that followed, Casper grew frail, and climbs up to the attic were more precious and made with the help of a cane. He used his study for longer stretches of time, thinking large thoughts and drawing important conclusions, occasionally pausing to gaze upon his radiant view of the Eden that never was. But invariably, after an intellectual afternoon spent in his chair, the air in his study would become stale. And Casper would pull himself up with his cane, work his way to the window, open the latch and feel the invigorating wash of fresh air rush past him, swirling through the room, and causing his eyes to tear as he gazed at the verdant hills that led to the ocean.

THE RING AND
THE COLLAR

F AR UP THE WINDSWEPT OREGON COAST, SURROUNDED BY
forested expanse, is a cozy two-bedroom masonry home. In the
backyard is a leash, tied to a deeply anchored stake. The trampled
arc swept by the leash inscribes the backyard and is most distinct at
the point closest to the back door. That is where Sharon and Phil, the
home's inhabitants, greet their black Labrador, Butch, who loves to be
outdoors, except when he is indoors. This has been their happy home
since shortly before Sharon and Phil were married two years ago.

The week before their wedding saw the final steps in an
undertaking that rivaled the raising of the Great Pyramid of Giza.
Legions had toiled for what seemed like decades to assemble
a ceremony fit for two who were everyone's best friends. The
penultimate stones had been heaved and put into place. All that
remained was the crowning stone. In Sharon's case, that was the
diamond from her grandmother's wedding ring. It would be placed in
a distinctive new gold setting, a braided loop designed by the couple
and crafted by a local artist, destined to adorn Sharon's finger forever
after Phil lovingly placed it there.

As the day approached, selected cadres handled the final, growing
threads of activities. One of those activities concerned the new ring.

Only the most senior legionnaire was trusted to execute this holy task. That legionnaire would unquestionably be Sharon's maid of honor, Cindy. She would be entrusted, deputized, to pick up the ring from the jeweler and deliver it to Sharon and Phil. The pyramid would be complete. The legions could drop their ropes to get cleaned and dressed in time for Saturday's ceremony.

On Friday morning, refreshed from a good night's sleep after Thursday's rehearsal dinner, Cindy drove to the jeweler's to retrieve the ring. The handoff was combined with good wishes from the jeweler. Cindy returned to her car, patted the shirt pocket to feel the ring, and then started down the two-lane road out of town. It wound through the forest under the everlasting slate gray skies. Satisfied at a job well done, she beamed and was pleased to arrive ahead of schedule before Sharon and Phil returned from the florist. What a fun surprise for them! She parked the car in the driveway, then walked to the unlocked back door and heard the dog's frenetic barking from inside. She let herself in, to Butch's rapturous welcome.

Seeing Butch's empty food bowl by the door, Cindy walked to the kitchen and grabbed the sack of kibble from under the sink. This locked Butch's attention and he tracked her as she bent over the bowl and poured the pellets. The resulting staccato built to the crescendo that Butch lived for. She stepped back and smiled as he took great gulps, his wagging tail not missing a beat. Moments later, his giant pink tongue zigzagged across the emptied bowl to search for elusive quantum kibble.

From the far side of the house, the garage door rumbled open, then, moments later, it rumbled closed. A door loudly shut and Sharon shouted, "Cindy! You're back already! Show me the ring!"

Thrilled, Cindy reached into her shirt pocket.

It was empty. She searched her other pockets. And searched them all again.

"Cindy?" came Sharon's nearing voice, now joined with a second set of footsteps. "Are you here?"

"Cindy!" Phil boomed.

The shout startled Cindy. Her thrill had left, leaving trepidation in its wake. She lurched for the back door, deftly turned the knob, and slinked out unnoticed.

Cindy leaned against the side of the house. The cold, wet, gritty brick and mortar wall made her shiver. But she had bought some time. She had to collect her thoughts. Moments later, in the background came the muffled staccato of another bowl of kibble being poured. At least Butch was having a good day.

Sharon scanned the yard through the back-door window, adjacent to the chilly wall against which Cindy was surreptitiously pressed. Cindy clenched her lip and the pain briefly distracted her from the cold and the fear.

"She's not out back," Sharon said to Phil.

They had seen her car out front, so she had to go in and face the music, music that would sound like a firing squad. She rehearsed alibis. *"The ring wasn't ready; I need to go back in a couple of hours." "A sign on the jewelry store door said they were out until noon."* She checked the shirt pocket again. Then she checked the others, turning them inside out, incredulous at the result.

She slowly backtracked her steps toward the car, around the side of the house, staring at the ground. She knew the ring hadn't just hopped out, but this wasn't about reason anymore.

Lost in this exercise, she heard a rapid tapping on a glass pane. She turned abruptly to see Sharon beaming at her from inside. Through the window, she could hear, "Hey! What are you doing out there? Come in and show me the ring!" Sharon emphasized the last detail by pointing to the blank location on her ring finger.

Time to come clean, she thought. Cindy wrenched a smile for Sharon and then trudged to the back door. Butch was bounding about loose in the yard and rocketed towards her. The impact knocked her onto the damp ground. "Get off!" she hollered as she pushed against the spastic canine hulk. The back-door burst opened and Sharon commanded the dog to come. Cindy rose, marked by paw prints, cold dampness, and mud.

"I am *so* sorry!" said Sharon, holding Butch by the collar. "He really loves you, but he should have been tied to his leash," which she then proceeded to do.

They stepped inside.

Sharon continued, "Why don't you get cleaned up, but first…" *Here it comes*, thought Cindy. "Show me the ring!" Phil was now beaming at her side.

Cindy's face whitened as she squirmed and blurted, "I had it." The response was utterly reflexive, employing no part of her brain above its reptilian core.

Sharon's smile froze, as if time stood still. Phil's expression morphed from jovial to quizzical. His face screwed up as he slowly said, "*Had* it?"

From a few millimeters above her frantic reptilian core, Cindy scrambled to compose a reply. Nothing came. Time to think. Sharon and Phil's eyes pierced her like icicles. "It was right here," she said, tapping her empty pocket. Phil and Sharon weren't biting. Cindy could practically see the twin question marks materialize over their heads. After a hundred thousand years, Phil said, "… and the other pockets?"

One hundred thousand years wasn't long enough. "I checked. Three times." Then, looking at Sharon, Cindy strained a smile, "And, oh Sharon, it looks beautiful!" Sharon's ice-smile thawed and collapsed like an avalanche. The exposed visage was stern and stony; cold, hard, immutable, and, most of all, unforgiving.

Phil took a breath. His intellect locked and loaded; Cindy could practically hear it click. Now Cindy was going to have to start dodging and weaving like a dimwitted rabbit. "If you had it in your pocket, where is it now? Why were you outside??" said Phil.

Ka-pow! The slug whizzed between Cindy's vertical ears. *Think, you idiot!* Now Sharon shifted from puzzled to skeptical. *Cut left! Cut right!* Sharon locked and loaded. "Cindy, where's my ring?" *Blam!* 16-gauge buckshot exploded the dirt in front of Cindy. Sharon and Phil reloaded.

Suddenly, the truth struck Cindy as quickly as she blurted it out. "It was in my shirt pocket before I fed Butch." She fell back into a chair and exhaled. It was curtains and she knew it. Finally, reason had managed to catch up to her mania, and lasso and rope it.

Phil's face matched Sharon's, like two looming, stone statues. "Where's Butch?" asked Phil, straining to contain his composure. Sharon and Cindy slowly pointed to the backyard.

The home was cozily nestled in the dense forest that, under normal circumstances, cultivated a spiritual serenity. This, of course, was shattered into fine shards when Sharon, Phil, and Cindy screamed, "Butch!" as they exploded out the back door.

Butch bounded toward the house, dragging his leash as he merrily galloped toward the three pained faces. Cindy grabbed Butch, who was so ecstatic with the affection that he once again slathered her blouse and slacks with paws laden with black mud from the recent rains.

Then they all stood and stepped back from the filthy, whirling dervish who barked hysterically, bluntly deprived of freedom and adoration.

Phil took a deep breath, pointed at Cindy, and said, "You." He started again. "You are going to pick through every piece of crap that comes out of that dog until you find the ring." Cindy stank of mud and didn't need to make eye contact with Phil. Staring at the crazy animal, she said, "I know."

Through all of this, Sharon silently stared into the forest. Tears streamed as she pondered the unthinkable. Her grandmother's diamond, mounted to the beautiful gold braided setting, was now in Butch's gut.

It started to rain.

Phil comforted Sharon as they stepped inside. Cindy turned to follow but Phil shot her a glance that made sifting through dog crap in the rain seem like the best deal available. The raindrops chilled and splashed and Butch started to whine. Cindy contemplated the pros and cons of feeding the dog a laxative.

Several shivering hours later, after Butch had made several deposits verified worthless by Cindy, one yielded dividends. Aided by a pocket comb (since disposed of) and a flashlight, Cindy finally extricated the ring while Butch relentlessly licked her ear. She gave a short prayer of thanksgiving when the diamond was found still in its setting. Cindy groaned as she stood and straightened. Her icy clothing wickedly clung everywhere and she reeked in ways only a dog would love, which Butch emphatically did.

Cindy put the ring in her pants pocket, grabbed Butch's collar, and unleashed him. She led the dog to the back-door window that looked into the dining room. There was evidence that a nice meal had been prepared and eaten. Butch yanked but Cindy held tight. Something had caught his attention; a blown leaf, perhaps. She knocked tentatively on the windowpane, leaving quartets of brown smudges. Butch yanked again, jerking her arm in painful, random directions. Cindy rapped louder and Phil materialized. As Butch gave a sharp jerk, Phil came to the window but Cindy had already blurted a "Stop it!" to Butch. Phil, thoroughly warmed by wine, overlooked it.

"I was talking to *him*, not you!" said Cindy. "I have the ring!" As rain streamed down her shivering face, she held the grimy ring up to the window. Phil managed a smile and opened the door, stepping back as Butch clambered in, euphoric memories of the outdoors instantly wiped from the dog's Etch-A-Sketch mind.

In the cozy confines of the space-heated home, Cindy stopped shivering but then started to reek. Butch shook himself frantically and Phil took several quick steps back as if at gunpoint, hands raised to avoid the vile spray.

"Keep it down!" slurred Phil in a loud whisper, "Sharon's asleep. A bit too much to drink... to steady her nerves." Then, staring at Cindy, he commanded, still smiling, "You, the dog, and the ring are taking a hot shower, then a hot bath... then another hot shower... and maybe another hot bath..."

"I get it," said Cindy. "Please start the water!"

"On second thought," Phil somehow reasoned through his stupor, "Gimme the ring. I'll clean it. You'd just lose it down the drain."

Cindy, incapable of pride or further humiliation, instantly produced the ring. "Keep it away from me."

Phil nodded in exaggerated agreement and gingerly gripped the fetid item between his thumb and index finger. He directed the maid of honor and dog to the guest bathroom.

Cindy was transfigured by a veritable waterfall of piping hot spring water, washed and soaked within clouds of soap and shampoo. Butch frolicked in the deluge and came clean au naturel.

In the kitchen, Phil scoured the ring in a bowl of hot water, with the aid of toothpaste, soap, and a soon-to-be-discarded toothbrush.

By the time he was done, Cindy appeared, layered in warm flannel. "Butch is asleep on his bed and I am going to mine," she said with a yawn. Gesturing at the dinner dishes, she said, "I will clean up this mess first."

"Don't worry," said Phil. "You earned the rest of the day off, but you'll be put to work again tomorrow." Then, with a glance at his watch, he added, "Oh wait, later today."

The night brought renewal. The hangovers that lingered were quickly vanquished by strong coffee, fresh air, and, above all else, the sight of the shining ring in a handy tray on the fireplace mantle. Sharon circled by that part of the house regularly to keep an eye on her treasure.

Hours later, the ceremony's rituals flowed lyrically without a single bad note. As ring bearer, Butch charmed the guests. The ring rested on a red satin pillow tied to his collar with a silver silk ribbon. Both dog and ring were remarkably squeaky clean. "What a good dog!" "Such a lovely ring!" Butch soaked up the praise. Cindy, trooper to the end, escorted her new quadruped friend.

The rest of the story is available for anyone to see in Sharon and Phil's wedding album, should you have the occasion to stop by to visit. Bring a treat for Butch!

IMMORTAL CHOICES

"THE USUAL," SAID ROGER.

"I don't know why I ask anymore." Mitch reached for the grocery store shelf and pulled down a can of De Soto brand creamed corn.

"How can anyone dislike corn?" said Roger. "It's so frigging basic."

They continued down the aisle, harvesting from the shelves.

"*Corn* is fine," said Mitch. With mock sternness, he shook the can with each phrase: "Corn on the cob, popcorn, petite white corn, you-name-it-corn, but…"

"Got it. Don't say it," said Roger. "Let's accept that this is the only difference between us. Identical twins, matched in every nuance except that you somehow cannot appreciate creamed corn."

Mitch smirked. "Matched. Right. Oh, except for diametrically opposite careers."

"Herr Professor," said Roger, with a slow and grandiose bow.

"Knock it off," barked Mitch to Roger's laughter as they proceeded to the checkout stand.

Once outside the store, they walked toward the bus stop. Roger whistled as Mitch carried the groceries, lost in thought. Suddenly, Mitch stopped and interrupted Roger's whistling with, "Hey, I can't go to the apartment now; I need to catch the subway to campus. There are some experiments and…"

"Never mind. Go," said Roger, taking the bag.

Mitch looked back as he strode away, "I won't be home for dinner."

Days, then weeks, flowed with familiar cadence as their two lives collided and coincided until one breezy Saturday afternoon in mid-summer.

The living room windows had been flung open and crosscurrents blew through. Roger was parked on the couch, again, iPhone gripped in his hand as he tapped the latest installment of interminable threads. Harry, their orange fluffy feline, was curled on the couch beside him.

Mitch walked in from his bedroom and stood in the center of the room. His eyes shined and he beamed expectantly at his oblivious brother.

"Yesssss?" Roger eventually hissed as he kept his gaze fixed on the device.

Acting as though he had an audience, Mitch cleared his throat and declared, "I adapted the Ergodic Hypothesis to the study of organisms."

"Meaning?" managed Roger, gaze unphased.

Waiting for Roger to decouple, Mitch said, "It's a bit complicated. Can you B-R-B?"

"Whatever," said Roger. He broke away from the screen and straightened his curled posture to face his brother.

Mitch resumed, with professorial delivery: "Consider the odds of a coin toss. To compute the odds of a toss coming up heads, I could flip a penny 100 times and count how many came up heads. Let's say, 52 times." Roger was still listening, so Mitch continued as he gestured to imaginary coin flips, "But we aren't done yet because a sample size of 100 is still small. If I had the time, and the patience, I could improve the accuracy by tossing hundreds or thousands of times more, counting as I go."

"What a *crushing* bore," said Roger.

"Indeed. But what if I had assistants to help?"

"You don't mean me, I hope."

Mitch took a breath. "No. But imagine if I paid ten people to each toss a penny 100 times. That's 1000 tosses."

He checked to confirm whether he still held Roger's fickle attention. Was Roger like a big fish fighting against his pull? Or like a caged animal ritually examining the perimeter of his cage, looping endlessly, mindlessly, in the vain hope of finding an opening? No, he was like Harry expecting a treat. And, when patience wore out, or a moth fluttered by, his attention would abruptly break.

Mitch persevered. "The number of heads from those 1000 tosses, even though they were spread across ten people, would be statistically the same as if one person tossed 1000 times, or 1000 people tossed once. That's an example of the Ergodic Hypothesis and I …"

Roger's phone vibrated. Moth. He was gone, reading a text message, typing a reply, and awaiting a response while the sun rose and set a million times over Mitch's stilled narrative.

Roger tucked the phone away and looked up. "Samantha."

"Shall I continue?" Mitch asked. Roger nodded, animated by his private exchange.

"That's the Ergodic Hypothesis. What would take the equivalent of millions of coin tosses can be collapsed into one grand coordinated coin toss." He paused for dramatic emphasis: "I figured out how to apply this principle to *biological systems*. Tests that would take days, weeks, or even *years* can happen in hours."

Alas, the emphasis was unrequited. Glancing up from his freshly retrieved phone, Roger asked, "Hmmm… so, how? I mean, why?" Back to the phone.

"The millions of coin tosses are millions of genetically identical cells, bred identically in identical environments. That was the tricky bit. But a million cells dividing once can now be mapped to one cell dividing a million times."

Now Mitch was pacing as he gesticulated. Roger glanced up, as Mitch announced, "That's *everything*! I have run accelerated experiments on cell longevity, *greatly* accelerated." He stopped before a small potted orchid. Cradling its petals, he continued, "I have run panels of tests with different drugs to see which ones extend cell life. And I can get very long term results, but overnight!" Roger stared at the orchid. As Mitch released the pedals, one fell to the floor.

Looking at it, Mitch continued, "Imagine if this plant could live for a thousand years." Then, looking back to Roger, "Imagine if you or I could."

Roger met his gaze. "That's astounding." He glanced down. "Have you tested it on anything beside germs?" He glanced up.

"Maybe we should discuss this some other time," said Mitch, the seething in his chest surging again. He could feel the veins standing out on his arms and hands.

"It's just that Samantha wants to get dinner with me tonight and…"

"Sure," said Mitch. "We can talk about it more later."

Roger bolted.

Mitch knew this drill well. Once again, he had been demoted to Harry's status, maybe lower; Roger would still have quality time with the cat. It was hopeless to bend the arc of Roger's new relationship. Patience was the order of the day, so he returned to his own obsession: The invention of immortality.

Mitch knew where he had to go; he had to make his temporary home on campus and take advantage of the relatively tranquil summer session. This would be his vacation. He exhumed an oversized suitcase from the closet where it had been buried. Tossing it on the bed, he filled it with clothes and sundries. He yanked a sleeping bag from a shelf, triggering a small avalanche, and found the inflatable sleeping pad. He ordered a cab, left Roger a note, and was gone before Roger returned from whatever he was up to.

In a laboratory storeroom, Mitch shoved boxes aside to make space for his bedding. He would sleep there surrounded by equipment, stacks of boxes, and plastic drums. Without a doubt, it was preferable to sharing a love nest—although, he thought, perhaps this was *his* love nest.

With the advantage of long-term experiments conducted each night, he tuned the drug's chemistry to exact stepwise improvements. After repeatable successes with microorganisms, it was applied to potted plants. The volley of experiments consumed much of the lab's stockpile of chemicals, but work became more efficient with

Mitch's understanding of the underlying molecular processes. Within two weeks of moving into the lab, successes were achieved with lab animals. This drew down most of the precious remaining supplies. Each improvement stretched lifespans further until, within a month, the results of long-term experiments were indistinguishable from immortality.

Stockpiles were exhausted. Sitting on the last drum of emptied chemicals, he stared at a test tube on the workbench in front of him. Too tired to stand, stamina depleted, the month of breakthroughs had yielded 10 CCs of a transparent, purple fluid. "Human grade immortality," he declared. Then, as he felt the month of tension suddenly unwind, he laughed out loud.

His laughter attracted a visitor. A door opened behind him and a fellow faculty member stepped in. "Mitch?" he asked. "What have you been up to?" The visitor grimaced as he surveyed the chaos and tried to fan away the chemical smells.

Mitch snapped out of his delirium, jumped up, and plugged the top of the test tube. He brushed past the visitor and shouted, "I'll be back later!" as he ran down the hall that was now streaming with students.

———

"Look what the cat dragged in," said Roger from the couch, glancing from his iPhone to his disheveled brother.

"Where's Samantha?" asked Mitch, as he looked around and caught his breath.

"Out."

Mitch took the test tube out of his pocket. "I just have enough for the two of us... and Harry." Roger looked at him, speechless.

Mitch continued, exclaiming, "But it has to be used soon, or it loses potency."

"Earth... to... Mitch," came Roger's deadpan reply.

Mitch focused his last wisps of energy to deliver the message: "Remember, right before I left, the Ergodic Hypothesis breakthrough?" He continued to catch his breath. "You asked whether I had tested it on anything beside germs?" Roger nodded his recollection. Mitch exclaimed, "I did it! What do you think I have been doing for the past month?"

"And what do you think *I* have been doing, *Herr Professor*?" laughed Roger.

Mitch frantically waved his hands to dismiss the non sequitur. Then he held out the test tube. "Do you want to live forever!?" he exclaimed, bracing for Samantha to barge in. He waited for one second and then declared, "I am going to take the dose. Right now." He gently placed the corked test tube on a chair, careful to make sure it wouldn't roll. From another pocket he pulled out a hypodermic syringe and pulled the cover off the needle. He flipped the cork off the test tube and, to Roger's horror, dipped in the needle and drew three CCs of the purple fluid into the syringe. He stuck the needle into his arm and pushed in the fluid.

Mitch closed his eyes. "I feel nothing, but I know... I know absolutely that this will work." He held out two fresh syringes in one hand and the test tube in the other. "Join me, Roger. This is all there is left and it will fade fast." He gestured to Harry, forever curled next to Roger, "He can come, too."

There was a tap-tap-tap at the door. "She doesn't have a key," whispered Roger in confidence to Mitch. "We aren't there in our relationship yet."

"Jesus, Roger! It's now or never!"

The voice from the door called out, "Roger? Who else is there?"

Roger looked at Mitch and stuck out his arm as he rolled up his sleeve, whispering, "Gimme." Then, as Mitch complied, Roger replied to Samantha, while flinching, "Hi! Mitch is here! Ouch!"

When it was over, he rolled down his sleeve, rising to the door. Mitch sat next to Harry, softly petting him, and did the deed, which elicited a yowl followed by a scampered escape.

---

150 years later, Mitch arranged to visit Roger in the old flat. He prepared for weeks and packed the intellectual baggage needed to cope with the increasingly foreign climate that Roger inhabited. "English," thought Mitch. "I'll have to speak in English."

The apartment building lobby was old and tired, but cared for. A wall that once hosted mailboxes had been resurfaced and now sported a nautical mural, ironically water stained from a ceiling leak. Mitch paced across linoleum that had faded along predictable traffic patterns. Avoiding the elevator, he mounted the stairs to the second floor and turned down the dim hallway. As he strode past the series of doors, each yielded distinctive sounds and smells, intermingling into a palpable expression of neighborhood. At his destination, Mitch faced the door and steeled his nerve to knock. The door's textured surface suggested layers of paint, an occasional chip exposing strata. Stacked on the hallway floor were empty food delivery boxes including, as expected, cartons of De Soto creamed corn and cat food. Playful tones and sound effects from a computer game danced through the door. Mitch shook his head, drew a breath, and knocked.

"Hey! Come in! It's unlocked," came the greeting.

Mitch opened the door, which pushed against a garbage bag that had been placed inside. The apartment smelled stale but not unclean. Looking past the cluttered kitchen, he saw into the living room and the source of the noise. Life-size holographic characters were engaged in hand-to-hand combat throughout the room, over and through the coffee table, chairs, and couch. Suddenly the sound stopped and the images froze and blinked away. From the couch, the back of Roger's head turned and he straightened a bit, "Welcome, bro! It's great to see you! My back is a bit messed up so I can't stand, but get over here!"

Mitch walked briskly to his brother, who lifted slightly from the couch. As they warmly embraced, Mitch noticed the weakness of Roger's hug and how his spine had developed a curve that rounded his shoulders. No matter, a brother was a brother. "Great to see you, too, man! You're looking good!" to which Roger issued a short laugh, before plopping back into the deeply worn couch. He was several inches shorter than Mitch recalled, as though the couch had been consuming him.

"Make yourself at home!" announced Roger.

The windows were shut tight and Mitch gazed out at the park across the street. In the mild afternoon, the park was animated with children, human exclamation points punctuating the cheerful scene.

Next to Mitch was a misplaced office chair on which rested a small cream-colored pillow. A crease cut across what would be the pillow's slouching belly had it been alive. One side of the cushion, the side that faced the window, was several tones lighter than the other. "Have a seat!" said Roger as he pointed a knobby finger toward the chair. Mitch wheeled the chair to face Roger and he picked up the pillow, which exposed bright-colored fabric hidden for perhaps a century. He swept the dusty chair and his hand imparted a small cumulous cloud that migrated into the room, sliced by the sunlight. He turned to look at his brother. "Oh dear," said Roger. "I really need to freshen the place up a bit."

Mitch said nothing as he brushed off his hands. He turned back to the chair and, despite its veneer of dust, sat. The chair creaked in response. Searching for a topic, he began with, "Well!" and then, "So, what ever became of Samantha?"

Roger smiled. "Oh, her? It was good while it lasted… 21? No, 22 years." He paused to recall ancient memories. "God, she got old. Didn't age well at all; too much sun worshipping, I guess." He gazed down and stroked Harry, curled up next to him on the couch in a spot compressed into a cat-shaped depression. Over the decades, Harry had become the fluffy filling of a convenient pothole. "Everything gets old, except Harry, my reruns and games, and me." Mitch demonstrably cleared his throat. "Oh, and you! But you don't count because you are never here," he said with disappointment that Mitch didn't read as genuine.

Eager to start a new chapter in an already hidebound conversation, Mitch cleared his throat again and then brightly asked, "What's next for you? Travel? Any backlog of projects or ventures?"

But Roger knew this chapter well. He knew the outline, the edits, and all revisions. He collected his thoughts and gestured with an unsteady sweep of his spindly arm as he said, "There are three chairs and one couch in this room."

"And several rooms in this apartment," Mitch asserted.

"Right, *Herr Professor*! And the basement garage… it should still be there," replied Roger, a dash of sarcasm added to an increasingly toxic brew.

Mitch closed his eyes but Roger was still there, continuing in a pedantic tone: "Now, I could sit on the chair over there where you are." Then he paused and pointed to the other chairs. "I could also sit on either of those." He took a breath. "And I *have*."

Mitch opened his eyes. Roger's claims were spoken like an explorer recounting visits to other continents. "I have sat at the *other* end of this couch, too," said Roger. "In fact, I tried that for a couple of years. My goodness! But, you know what, Mitch?" Roger paused, waiting for an acknowledgement he knew was not going to come before he delivered his insightful conclusion: "I like *this* end of the couch."

Q.E.D., thought Mitch.

"My table is here," Roger said, tapping it, and looking to his side at the cat in the pothole, "…and Harry likes it here."

"No backlog, I guess," said Mitch.

"No," stated Roger, as though he was making a point.

Mitch stood, brushed off his pants, and started toward the door. "I am getting on your nerves."

"Wait," said Roger. "Please stay. Sit down." He cobbled together sentiment from old scraps of curiosity and empathy. "Um, so, what have you been up to?"

Mitch sat back in the chair, incredulous. "Well, I would be glad to… I don't want to bore you…" Roger appeared genuinely interested, so Mitch continued, "I have several projects. I work on one until I reach an impasse, then I jump to another. Eventually, each one advances. It keeps me busy."

That word "busy" snagged Roger like a fishhook, a painful rusty fishhook that he wished would go away. He wanted Mitch to stop, but managed to say, "What project are you working on now?"

Mitch's face glowed. "Oh, it's great! Let's see… you know how the inside of the lung is coated with short, hairlike cells called 'cilia'?"

Roger's face turned quizzical. Mitch continued: "They flick impurities out of the lung, keeping it nice and clean."

"OK…" said Roger, cautiously, worried where this fishhook was going to drag him.

"Imagine if carpeting could function like cilia, just covering the floor of a house. Imagine that each carpet fiber was *powered* and that waves of pulses in the carpet flicked the dust and debris toward a vacuum port." Checking, he saw from the look of shock that Roger was still engaged. "Then the house would *cough* to eject the dust or perhaps, maybe better, the dust would be bagged up nicely. I am still working that part out." He looked at the grayed carpet around him. "Good lord, cilia carpeting in this apartment would be great."

"Yeah, I get it," said Roger with a smirk. He turned on the hologram game. Several battling characters materialized between the brothers, fists and clubs swinging as the room filled with gaudy music and sound effects.

"Do you get it, Roger?" Mitch yelled through the brawl that surrounded him. He stood. "Do you really? Because I am not sure you have room up there," he said as he tapped his temple. "How many thousands of reruns can the human brain store? How do you manage to catalog them all?"

"No problemo," yelled Roger. His jaw tightened as he fixated on the game and commanded the characters to face Mitch. They lifted their clubs, demonic eyes burning.

Mitch continued, now that the flood gates were open: "And the games?!" he hollered. "How do you manage to keep track of the rules, the levels, the characters, and the strategies?" His yelling caused Harry to stir and he peeked at him.

Roger's face flushed. "Maybe you want them all swept out?" and he commanded the brutes to pummel Mitch with their virtual weapons. "*Not a chance!*" was Roger's battle cry.

"It's your life!" yelled Mitch. He strode towards the door through the bludgeoning fiends and then over the garbage bag. Turning back, he shouted, "But *live it!*" He slammed the door behind him and a little vortex of dust swirled in its wake.

Roger clenched his eyes to block any tears and took several deep breaths. Then, composed, he resumed his game of Grave Robbers as the dust settled.

Mitch stood in the hall as his every nerve vibrated. He caught his breath, his heart surged, and echoes of the game bled into the hallway. How could this have possibly gone worse? Instead of packing the necessary intellectual baggage, it was as though he had packed only a toothbrush for a visit to the Arctic. What a fool.

The game noise stopped. Inside the apartment, Mitch heard, "C'mon Harry," followed by shuffling.

Mitch steadied himself and collected his thoughts. He couldn't leave like this. He waited, then cracked open the door. "Roger?"

Silence.

"Can I come in?" he asked.

"Come in," came the eventual flat response from somewhere deep in the apartment.

Mitch entered and found the living room empty. He walked down the short hallway to the master bedroom. He cracked open the door and poked in his head into the darkened room.

"What do you want?" barked Roger. "You'll just be disappointed."

Maybe it was not time to build fences yet. "Going down for your nap?"

Through the dim light Roger stared at Mitch before closing his eyes and turning away. Mitch turned to leave, closing the door behind him. Harry sat on the hallway runner and, seeing a door close, promptly requested it to be opened. The request was in the form of a sideways rub against Mitch's ankle as Harry slinked past him and toward the door. Mitch cracked the door open and Harry poured into the darkness.

Mitch felt bile simmer in his chest as he walked toward the living room. He stopped to survey the scene. Straight, well-worn paths connected the kitchen, bathroom, master bedroom, and, of course, the end of the couch that had the large and small dents. A lesser path led from the couch to the cat's bathroom and its litter box mounted over the toilet. And that was it. That was the God's eye view of Roger's existence, the map of his efficiently compressed world.

Mitch slowly shook his head. The bile welled up and displaced the momentary tranquility, squeezing that out with each deepening breath until his full body quietly seethed. "He's already asleep by now; almost certainly sound asleep." He imagined Harry curled up next to Roger. How could that peaceful scene upset him? Now he was upset because he was upset. He wished there was a master switch to shut off these voices.

"Enough," he affirmed. He strode to the office chair and flung away the creased pillow. He swiveled the chair, aimed it toward

117

the bedroom, and pushed. "Hey, Roger!" No response, as the chair wheeled down the hallway.

He knocked, then opened the bedroom door.

"What the hell!?" exclaimed Roger, struggling to rise up on his elbows. In the commotion, Harry hopped down and ducked under the bed.

"We are going out!" announced Mitch. "It's a beautiful day! Oh, it's a little cloudy, but …"

"You are out of your mind!" barked Roger. "Get out!"

"That is the smartest thing you've said all day. Let's get out!" replied Mitch as he barged further into the room and pulled open the drapes. Roger, shielding his eyes from the light, pivoted to kick Mitch but the blankets weighed down his legs. Smiling, Mitch reached down to bundle up his helpless brother.

Mitch pulled Roger's atrophied body from the bed. There was so little left of him, thought Mitch, as his weak brother vainly struggled. "Calm down," said Mitch. "You'll thank me later."

"Bastard," spat Roger. Mitch placed him on the chair and pulled off the bedding to reveal that Roger had napped fully clothed. Roger winced as his malformed body sank into a chair shaped for someone with normal posture. Too weak to resist, he clung to the chair as Mitch pushed it quickly out of the bedroom, past the kitchen, and into the second floor hallway. "Stop. I'm scared."

Mitch ignored the plea and pressed on. He briskly moved the chair down the hallway as Roger looked around at mundane sights not seen in years. The chair stopped abruptly in front of the elevator, causing Roger to dig his fingers in deeper. "I am here," Mitch assured him, "It's OK. We are just going outside." He pushed the button and the elevator promptly arrived.

"Yeah, *Herr Professor*, you're here. That's why I'm terrified."

The elevator opened and Mitch rolled in the chair. Moments later, they were in the lobby, moving past the nautical mural, and then outside.

"Holy crap," said Roger, as sunlight blasted his face and a cool breeze washed around him. He wheezed as fresh air shocked his lungs. His hands trembled. Mitch didn't notice as he pushed the chair across the sidewalk and, after a pause for traffic, across the street.

Mitch laughed as he declared, "What doesn't cure you will kill you!" They entered the park.

Roger didn't respond.

Mitch pushed the chair to a spot where Roger could see the children on the slide and swing set. "See what you're missing?"

Roger's head slowly hung down. His hands relaxed their grip and fell.

Mitch turned to his brother. "Rog—?" He dropped to a knee to look up at Roger's face. His brother's chin now rested on his chest, eyes shut. He gripped Roger's wrists to search for a pulse and urgently called his name again... and again.

Roger was still.

As children turned toward the scene, Mitch, face flushed, paused, wiped his eyes, then stood.

"It's his nap time," he announced.

As hot tears streamed, Mitch turned the chair and slowly rolled him back.

A tide of grief engulfed Mitch. It changed the landscape like the force of nature that it was. He felt like he would drown and never touch bottom, but eventually, mercifully, the grief started to ebb. It receded slowly, easing away until finally, once again on emotional terra firma, Mitch could resume the life that had been utterly displaced.

The decades that Mitch and Harry then spent together accumulated into centuries. Mitch saw creative horizons and crossed them. He climbed intellectual mountains to see the more distant horizons that beckoned. Wherever these endeavors took them, whatever Mitch's scientific or artistic achievements, Harry remained content to stretch out in the warm sunlight, even if it was from another star, and forever repeat the few steps of his life's routine. When this would remind Mitch of his brother, tears and anger might return, but only briefly, as his love for Roger was immortal.

AUTHOR BIO:

Brad Ashmore has been a technologist, animated film creator, inventor, and writer (not necessarily in that order). He lives in Silicon Valley with his wife, two kids, and a bad cat. When he is not at "Shut Up & Write" Meetups, he can be found in coffee shops writing or working on his next gadget. Brad also can be found at "UnexpectedBooks.com".

www.ingramcontent.com/pod-product-compliance
Lightning Source LLC
Chambersburg PA
CBHW030544130626
46552CB00006B/2418